SYRIA GIRL

Syria Girl

ELIJAH HILL

DFM Publishing

"Over 5.6 million people have fled Syria since 2011, seeking safety in Lebanon, Turkey, Jordan and beyond. Millions more are displaced inside Syria and, as war continues, hope is fading fast."

THE UNITED NATIONS REFUGEE AGENCY

"If people were rain, I was drizzle and she was a hurricane."

JOHN GREEN, LOOKING FOR ALASKA

THE END

(And also the beginning)

It was Friday, a school day, and once again I was stuck in court.

I wore ripped jeans, a baggy hoodie, and a slightly muddy pair of converse sneakers. It was meant to be a joke – they were the same clothes I'd worn breaking into the bottle store.

The stiff-looking lawyer they'd assigned me didn't seem to get the punchline though.

'This is your third time meeting Streisand,' he whispered to me as he ruffled through his case notes, 'You know what she's like.'

I ignored the twat and looked around the small courtroom. Two eyes glared back at me. The bottle store owner was trying to be a tough guy. I snorted and glared back until his stare shifted away. I glanced at the police prosecutor, some old dude with a big moustache, and then up front where the court aide was getting to her feet.

'All rise for Judge Streisand.'

I heard heels clicking on the oak floorboards. We stood. The lawyer was sighing. My feet started to heat up. I moved my weight from one foot, and back to the other.

I'm done for.

The clicking heels grew louder and more prominent, and then bursting through the double doors was Judge Margaret Streisand. She had a hawk's nose and hawk eyes.

'Scared?' my lawyer whispered.

I shrugged. 'She just acts like she's disappointed in me you know? No one else does that.'

Judge Streisand didn't look at me as she strolled past. Instead, she said hello to the police prosecutor, checked in with her court staff, then pulled out a stack of paperwork from behind her desk. I wanted to run away. I could feel my muscles tensing up.

I won't make it through the door, I thought, *But so what? I shouldn't have come in the first place.*

The judge finished consulting with whoever needed consulting, gave her paperwork a slight rustle, then declared court open. I shut my eyes.

'Mr Danny Frey.' She boomed from the front of the room, 'I thought we'd made a deal.'

I opened my eyes. *Everyone* was staring at me, 'Sorry miss.'

'*Sorry?* Sorry works the first two times you come to court. As they say in the U.S – third strike and you're out.'

I stared at the picture of the Queen, and the Union Jack that sat behind her desk; trying to avoid those eyes.

'Anyway....' she shook her head, 'Let's hear what the police have to say.'

As usual, the police prosecutor mumbled his way through what had happened. There was security footage of a group throwing bricks through the bottle store windows before helping themselves to what was inside.

One of the youths was wearing the same jersey I'd been found in. Three bottles of scotch had also been found on me (there'd been a fourth but I disposed of the evidence at a party the night before). The total cost of the theft ran to around £2000 – not a big deal, but the fact that I'm not rich and this was my third time sort of made it a big deal.

When the prosecutor had finished, the bottle store owner spoke. Then my lawyer spoke. Then the police prosecutor said something which my lawyer refuted and they all descended into a technical-term festival.

I was struggling to stand still. I needed to run or have a fight or jump off a pier or something. My eyes flicked about; I noticed a rather large woman walking through the court doors. She wore a white hat with a red cross on it and when she caught Streisand's eye the judge smiled which was something I'd never seen before.

The red cross lady squeezed into one of the aisles and stared at me. She looked like she wanted to smile at me or something so I turned away and pretended to watch my future being decided. When I looked back she was still watching me.

Back in the realm of court decisions, things were happening too fast for me to keep up. The judge finished with the police, my lawyer, and the liquor store owner, and concentrated her full attention on me. I gulped again, wondering if it was still too late to run.

'Mr Frey,' she said, 'The police *and* your lawyer have mentioned that there were other youths on the scene with you.'

I stared ahead, not looking at her.

'Mr Frey,' she repeated, 'You could cut the time of your sentence if you were to add a few names to our list.'

I stood silent, she had to ask me again, 'Well?'

'I don't rat.'

'Even for a reduced sentence?'

'Even for a reduced sentence your honour.'

She gave a sharp nod.

'How old are you Danny?'

'I'm seventeen your honour.'

'Well right now you're not making many smart moves. This is your third offence and what's stopping you from committing another?'

She paused, waiting for me to speak, I just crossed my arms and stared towards the ceiling. When I didn't answer she looked across at my lawyer, 'At the moment your jail sentence is looking like six months in juvenile detention.'

I tried to keep a straight face, but inside I was kicking myself for not bursting into tears or something. A few of my mates had been to juvie and they all came out colder.

Streisand stared around the courtroom, 'Six months of juvenile detention, there's no telling what a young man will learn there... It could scare them off a life in crime, give them a deterrent. Or it can harden them. Push them over the edge.'

She paused like the narrator of a play... letting her sentence roll out to fill the courtroom.

'But Mr Frey, I also have a second option on display today.'

Judge Streisand turned to the large woman in front, the one who'd been watching me.

'Donna Appleby from the Red Cross has alerted me to a new youth program they're running.'

The judge pulled out a sheet of paper and read from it, 'The scheme takes young juvenile delinquents to places where they can do some good. In two weeks, Donna will be heading to Turkey to work in a refugee camp housing people affected by the Syrian civil war.'

I stared at this Donna woman; she was nodding along. Then her eyes flicked to me and she smiled. I pretended I hadn't made eye contact by turning back to the judge.

'In five months you'd be finished Mr Frey, so this is shorter than your juvenile detention sentence, but still long enough to have an impact on your life.'

She peered over her glasses at me, 'What do you think?'

My lawyer put his hand up like he wanted to say something, but I beat him to it – anything was better than juvie.

'I'll do it.'

What could have been a smile twitched on her lips, 'Is our police prosecutor happy with that?'

The policeman consulted with a deputy before nodding.

'Very well then,' said Judge Streisand, 'I hereby hand Mr Frey over to the Red Cross.' She hardened her tone, 'If you ever turn up here again Mr Frey, you'll be serving everything in full. We want you to be able to contribute to society Mr Frey, but this is your last chance to come clean.'

I nodded, 'Thanks, your honour.'

Then my lawyer and I were walking out of there, halfway down the aisle, the Red Cross woman stepped out in front of me.

'Nice to meet you Danny,' the woman gave a big wide motherly sort of grin, 'Our plane leaves from Heathrow the Monday after next, I'll be in touch.'

'Thanks,' I grunted, and as my lawyer and I walked off I was thinking about the bullet I'd dodged. There were worse prison wardens than the Red Cross lady.

But one thing made me pause for a moment as my lawyer hailed a cab.

Where the hell is Turkey?

****

The tarmac was hot, blurry, and cracked despite it still being midway through spring.

Our plane had just touched down at Izmir Adnan Menderes Airport, Turkey, and we were transferring our luggage from the terminal to an old Land Rover with safari covers.

We were a group of eight, all British, all carrying pale complexions and sweating like crazy even though we'd only been outside for about two minutes.

Donna, the large Red Cross minder I'd seen in court, sat in the passenger's seat. While a tall but lanky middle eastern man hopped into the driver's side. Both wore the red cross on the chest of their t-shirts.

I piled into the back with the other juvies and sat staring out the window. I don't think any of us really knew what to do with each other. In prison, we would've established some sort of pecking order, but this was different.

Sitting in the row across from me was a girl with long dreads and a tattoo rolling across her shoulders. She raised her eyebrows, 'What are you here for?'

It was a typical juvie question, 'I robbed a bottle store.'

'Seems harsh you'd get this.'

'It was my third strike.'

She nodded, exposing the silver on her teeth, 'I shot my drug dealer in the kneecap.'

'Now *that* seems harsh.'

'Well,' she said, a vicious smile playing across her lips, 'It was *his* third strike.'

The rest of the juvies were the same as dreadlocks girl, slightly psychopathic teens with bad upbringings and broken homes. The Land Rover was filled with swearing, a couple of gang references, and bragging as it made its way to the place we were supposed to be helping out.

A large fence wormed its way around the camp, but the fence had no gates. Donna explained to us that people were free to come and go as they pleased.

'Most stay though,' Donna said, 'Good jobs are scarce and it's hard to get back on your feet when your life has been swept from under you.'

Around us, there were hundreds and hundreds of tents made up of more colours than I'd ever imagined. I laughed as I spotted a Homer Simpson tent. The girl next to me turned her dreadlocked head, 'What's funny?'

I pointed out the tent and she cracked up, 'Of all places for that fat American to show up....'

The Land Rover rolled to a stop outside the barracks we'd be staying in. The setup was nothing more than a group of shipping containers with a canvas roof stretched over top of them. There were four bunks to a container plus area to store our stuff.

It'd barely make one-star accommodation in the U.K, but in the camp, it was a mansion when compared to the Homer Simpson tent.

We were told to choose any bunk we wanted, I was a little slow and ended up with one of the bottom bunks near the window. It suited me just fine: heat rises, and we'd be there through the summer, top bunk wouldn't be quite so enjoyable at that point.

As I was setting up my bed, the girl with the dreads watched. She had the bottom bunk at the other side of the container.

'Whereabouts in the U.K are you from?' she asked.

'London, you?'

'Edinburgh.'

I nodded and went back to my bed, I didn't see the point in small talk, we'd have enough time to get to know each other over the next five months.

'What's your name?'

'Huh?'

'I said what *the hell's* your name?'

'Danny.'

I didn't need to ask her name, she'd tell me.

'I'm Malia.'

I sat down, the bed creaked, 'It's a crazy place we've found ourselves in.'

She shrugged, then spat in the corner of the room, 'Beats juvie.'

I nodded, and looked outside at the rows of tents that flapped in a slight wind, 'Yeah... for us anyway.'

****

When we'd finished setting up Donna called us from the kitchens. We all filed out to where she sat waiting.

In fact, it was only the second time I'd seen Donna sitting. The whole way to Turkey she'd been rushed off her feet organising us. Now it seemed she could lighten the load a little.

'So, we made it. You managed to fly more than 4200 kilometres and sit through the drive here without killing each other. We may have hope for the coming months.'

I stared around, killing was probably the wrong phrase to bring up in front of a group of juvenile delinquents.

Still, Donna's energy and motherliness seemed to sweep most of the group over. Rows of silver teeth and scarred cheeks smiled at her.

'Once we've eaten, we'll head into the camp so you can see what it's like. Then we'll have a chat about the shower block we're going to be installing.'

After eating tender, spice-infused, Turkish kebabs we shuffled from the shade of the containers into the heat of the camp. Up close the tents weren't quite so vivid, most of the colour had been bleached from them by the sun.

Men, women, and children sat outside. Young mothers nursed babies.

Just like in England a group of young boys played football, only their stained leather ball was hardly recognisable from the synthetic fabrics we'd use at home, and not one of the little boys with their shirts off had any fat on their bones.

Our group cheered when one kid with a shaved head and only one arm volleyed the ball into their goal – two Red Cross flags about a meter and a half apart.

We stopped in an area just past where the boys were playing, it was inside the perimeter fence but had no tents on it.

'We're looking at installing a new temporary shower block.' Donna said. 'Everything in this camp is meant to be temporary, but some of these people have been here for years.' she wiped a patch of sweat from her cheek, 'No one's really got a clue what to do with them.'

'So, when I say a temporary shower block it means it needs to last a long time, but appear to be removable.'

She turned to us, 'This is where you come in my English ambassadors, particularly those of you with a bit of muscle. You'll be installing these *temporary* shower blocks.'

Malia – the girl with the dreads bumped me with her shoulder, 'What do you think?'

I shrugged, 'At least we're not cleaning toilets.'

She laughed, a large unfiltered sort of cackle. I found myself grinning, 'You?'

Malia rolled up her shirt sleeve, revealing yet more tattoos and a solid bicep. 'See these guns here... They were built for two things... fighting and construction.'

She snorted, then spat on the dusty ground.

We made our way to the toilet block, hell on earth, despite modern materials, and the Red Cross' best efforts, flies buzzed around the buildings like vultures.

Other departments we toured were the ration hall, gear centre, camp operations and finally the field hospital. A set of tall white tents housed metal bunks and an orchestra of coughs, groans, and screams.

The place was hot and stank of disinfectant. The nurses went around with bags of ice, placing them on patients' heads, and adjusting the lines of morphine into their veins.

Donna started strong as she talked about the horrors some of the people had faced, and the countries providing aid and taking the wounded in. But the further we walked that white tunnel of despair the less she had to say until it seemed the only reason we were moving forwards was because it would've taken longer to go back the way we came.

Finally, we emerged from the hospital and gulped in breaths of disinfectant-free air.

'Whatever you do guys,' said one of the juvies, 'Don't get sick, because I ain't coming to visit you.'

****

Night fell but the temperature almost seemed to rise. My heart felt like it was thumping out of my chest. I kept thinking about snow – the cool English snow. Someone in our cabin was snoring. I tossed the blanket off my bed and rolled onto my stomach with a groan. Through the window rows of tents reflected the starlight.

'That's it,' I whispered, 'I can't sleep.'

I stood and nearly tripped on my blanket. I whispered a couple of swear words to myself and tugged my boots on.

The door of our container slid open without a squeak. I spotted the soldier guarding us half asleep behind a cigarette. His feet dangled near my head as I crouched past him and the sand masked my footsteps as I moved into a run.

The tents flashed past. Some of them glowed with faint colour. The fresh air seemed to cool around me.

At the edge of the camp, I spotted the outline of the water tower, and even before I consciously thought about climbing it, my legs and hands were pulling me up the ladder. I blinked and I was three stories high, sitting on top of a concrete tank with my legs dangling over the edge.

I laughed into the night sky. Tents glowed below me while a cluster of city lights twinkled off on the horizon. The energy of the night and the cool made my arms shake. I wanted to fight, to steal something, or ride a motorcycle as fast as possible.

I looked over the edge of the water tank, it was high enough to be dangerous.

I slid over the side until I was just hanging onto the edge with my hands, my feet dangled far from the uneven ground below.

I considered letting go and felt the thrill of adrenaline.

Then I heard a shuffling sound above me. There was barely time to say 'huh?' before two feet appeared an arm's length to my right, then legs, shoulders, and a silhouette of a face.

'Hello there,' the face said, its voice was warm with an Arabic accent.

My mouth opened, but I didn't know what to say.

'I don't usually get visitors up here,' the girl flicked the long silk hair that ringed her face, she waited a moment before continuing, 'Are you usually this silent, or have I picked the wrong language?'

She switched to Arabic.

'I'm Danny,' I said, my forearms were beginning to ache, 'Aren't you scared of falling?'

Her white teeth flashed in the dark. She carefully took one hand from the edge and held it out to me.

'Are you?'

She was holding on with a single hand, I looked down, the ground was too far to drop without breaking a leg. But then there was this girl. I didn't know what to think. So instead I just did.

I reached out my right hand and touched hers. Her fingers curled between mine. They were warm and steady. My left hand shook and sweated as it clung to the tank. I felt myself begin to slip.

'Maybe we should just let go?' she laughed.

Vertigo hit my stomach and I let go of her hand, then tried to scramble up the side of the water tower. My knee banged the side, and I felt my shin tear. My arms shook as I edged my elbows, then my stomach back onto the flat, safe, top.

I was panting as the girl calmly pushed herself up beside me.

'I'm sorry,' she said, 'I get caught up in the fun sometimes. You were very brave to hang off the edge like that.'

I stared at her, trying to find words.

She reached out a hand and touched my shoulder, 'I'm sorry,' she said again and in the same breath she was on her feet and walking towards the ladder. There was this slight tapping as she descended. I stood up and walked to the edge of the ladder and searched for her, but all I could see was the ground. Somewhere in the distance, I could hear an Arabic lullaby echoing through the tents.

I hung around and tried to imagine what I should've said to her. Slowly the night grew colder and when the words wouldn't come, I snuck back to the containers and lay back in my bed just staring at the bunk above me.

****

We spent the day shifting timber and pipes for the new shower block.

A couple of refugee guys wandered over and picked up spades. They were quiet. Almost depressed as they moved. Their skin shone in the sun. I looked into their eyes and they nodded to me.

Sometimes they sang. Sometimes they laughed. But always those moments were tinged with sadness.

We managed to dig a couple of holes in the sandy earth and put in round bits of wood and concrete. The work was hard, and as night rose my mind wandered from work to home to the girl on the water tower.

During dinner I drank six cups of water, then packed myself off to bed. A couple of hours later I woke, took a slash, then slipped out the window.

My bare feet touched the sandy ground with a light thud.

In the distance, I could see the water tower. Right in the centre was a small silhouette of shoulders, a head, and a thatching of long hair.

I ran, took the ladder two rungs at a time and sat down beside her with my legs dangling over the edge.

I looked at her, it was the same girl from the night before, although I could only see her smile and her eyes catching the stars as she gazed off into the horizon.

I cleared my throat, 'You live in the camp?'

The girl rolled her eyes, 'Why else would I be here?'

I shrugged, 'I'm helping to build the new shower block.'

'So, you volunteered?'

'Well...' I thought about juvie, and the way the glass had fractured into a million pieces as I'd thrown a brick through the bottle store window, and I almost told the truth.

But then there was a flash of light in the distance and it illuminated the girl's face and I saw she had the perfect lips, and eyes that seemed to be smiling at me.

'Yeah, I volunteered.'

She nodded, 'If you stare far enough into the horizon you can almost see it.'

'See what?'

'See England – your home.'

I gazed at the black and darkness out beyond the camp. I couldn't really see anything. But then I felt her hand reach into mine. I closed my eyes and focused on the warmth of her fingers as she traced her thumb along the back of my hand.

She coughed, 'My name's Ayamin. And one day I'm going to England.'

I turned to her and just stared at her face as she gazed out trying to see London in the darkness. I lifted her hand to my lips and watched the almost-laughing smile that appeared when I kissed the back of it.

****

'Come on, just a little peek?'

'No.'

'I promise I won't say anything.'

'Danny...'

A week had passed. We lay on the top of the water tank on a blanket Ayamin had brought from her tent. I lay facing north, and her head was resting on my shoulder so our faces were close and we could see the stars.

'I want to see your tent,' I said again.

'But why?' she was shaking her head.

'Because... I don't know... I guess I just want to know you as more than the girl on top of the water tank.'

'You'd rather know me as the girl who lives in an undersized kids' tent?'

I touched the side of her face, 'I'd rather know you as you.'

She screwed up her face like she was deciding whether to push me off the tower or not, before sighing and staring down at her feet.

'Danny, what are we doing?'

'What do you mean?

'I mean what are we doing here?'

'Well I'm lying on my back looking at the stars, and your head is on my shoulder, and I'm trying not to give it away, but my arm's dead.'

She laughed and moved her head back slightly. Her hand touched the side of my face and gently turned my head so her eyes were looking into mine.

'I mean Danny, you're going to go back to England. Someday soon you'll go back to your life and I'll go back to what's left of mine.' Her fingers traced along the line of my jaw then slipped down to my chest, 'Why are we here, now, Danny? I know it's only been a week, but if we carry on like this it's only going to be painful when one of us leaves.'

I stared into her eyes. Took a breath, then another, and then another.

She moved her face closer to mine, the tips of our noses touched, and she smiled.

'Hello? Danny? Is your brain home?'

I laughed, moved closer, and touched my lips to hers.

'Yeah, my brain's home. He's just a little slower than most,' I wiggled so I was facing the sky again, 'Personally, I'm more of a *go with the flow* kind of guy. I think if you're always waiting for the future to happen you never really get to enjoy yourself.'

I felt her shrug beside me, 'Refugees only have the future. Hope that things are going to get better is about the only thing most of us own.'

'Shit, you're right. Forget everything I just said.'

She laughed into my shoulder, and then kept her head there. Pressed into me, facing away from the world.

I brushed a hand through her hair.

'Still, you were talking about hope, right? How about the hope that we'll see each other again? Maybe you'll end up in England? Maybe I can get a job when I get back. I'll pay for your visa. I'll pay for your flights. Hell, I'll even fund your ice-cream addiction.'

Ayamin's laugh flooded through my chest. And when she looked up, there were two little streaks of tears on my t-shirt.

'Danny!' Her mouth pushed against mine and her hands pulled against my shirt and her hair was falling all over my face and I could hardly breathe for all her passion.

'God. Danny. You say some stupid things.' She muttered as she pulled away, 'But they make me want to dream.'

She sat up, 'Okay, I'll take you to my tent... But if you want to see inside, first you have to meet my grandma.'

****

Ayamin had a novel, a bunch of poppies, and a jar of water in her arms when I met her beside the hospital.

She glanced both ways then pulled me into a hug.

'Hi,' her hand found mine and we pushed through the white plastic doors into the hospital.

The smell of disinfectant hit me so hard I nearly staggered back out.

Ayamin winced, 'I suppose you're not used to it yet.'

I took another breath and tried to stop myself from retching, 'Do you ever get used to it?'

'Depends how much time you spend here... besides the disinfectant is only there to hide its true smell.'

She started walking down the rows, and I followed her, glancing at the people who rested under slightly stained white hospital sheets. Needles and drug lines dripped into veins, and moans and coughs escaped their lips.

Our feet had only been tapping on the plywood floors for a minute when Ayamin stopped in front of a shrunken old lady with wispy black hair and an almost toothless smile.

'Aya!' The woman chirped. Ayamin put the book on the woman's bedside table and the red and yellow poppies in the jar of water. She kissed her grandma on the cheek, and as Ayamin stood back up the old woman tugged on her jacket with a shaky hand, and whispered to her in Arabic. The old woman's eyes went from Ayamin to me, and back again.

Ayamin laughed, and her face went red. She turned to me, 'Danny, would you like to meet Grandma Teete?'

Teete's hand touched my cheek as I knelt in front of her, she raised her eyebrows to Ayamin and nodded her head.

'Good.' she murmured, and then said another sentence in Arabic that made Ayamin screech with laughter. Ayamin shook a finger at her grandma and the two of them exchanged super-fast sentences in Arabic that set them both laughing.

Ayamin's laugh was light and warm, and her grandma's was the same, only rougher. The old woman put a hand to her chest and started to cough. Gradually Ayamin's laugh faded as Grandma Teete's cough grew louder and louder. We sat in silence as her grandma wiped the flecks of spit and red splotches of blood from her elbow.

There was silence.

'Your book on the table, it looks interesting' I said, more to get the sound of coughing out of our minds than anything else.

Ayamin picked it up, it had a yellow mountain daisy on its cover. Its pages were worn and dog eared from use. She flicked through it and a small smile ventured back onto her face.

'It's called *Two Hearts in The French Night*. It's our favourite book.' she laughed, 'Teete says it helps her to believe she can still find love.'

She rubbed her grandma's shoulder and the old woman nodded.

'Usually I'd read to her. You don't have to but... if you want to stick around and hear...'

I picked up a white plastic hospital chair, put it down beside her, and took a seat.

'I wouldn't miss it for the world.'

A faint smile crept onto her lips as she began to read. The book was in English but she spoke in Arabic for Grandma Teete. I enjoyed her voice – it was almost musical. I enjoyed the way she folded her hair behind her ear and the slight lift in her voice when she came to one of her favourite parts. At one point she put the book aside and read two chapters with her eyes closed – straight from her memory. I guess that's how important the book must have been to her. Or at least how many times she'd read it.

Samantha sat on the steps of the church waiting. The lights of Briancon were dark to save electricity – she had only the moon to find Rudy.

She wondered why he'd come to the small mountain town in the first place. She wondered why he'd stayed. She wondered where he was tonight. The moon was far above the church's tiled roof.

As she read, I began to feel something in my heart, it was like waking up from a deep sleep, it happened slowly at first and then bam. I was awake. Maybe it was love. Maybe it was the smell of disinfectant.

I heard a cough and looked up, Ayamin was not the only one being watched. Grandma Teete's eyes flicked to me and she had this not-so-subtle grin on her face.

The sound of Ayamin replacing the bookmark was like the closing of a dream. She smiled at her grandma, and turned to me, 'You enjoy that?'

'When's the next session?'

She raised her eyebrows to Grandma Teete who winked.

Ayamin rolled her eyes, 'We read again on Thursday.'

'Count me in.'

****

That week I volunteered to carry messages around the camp. It meant I got to explore – and spend more time with Aya. As the long hot days wore on, I began to realise how different our lives were.

I realised by Friday that Ayamin wore the same three pairs of clothes in rotation – a mix of mostly reds, greens, and yellows. It took me a little longer to understand that she only had those three pairs of clothes.

I realised just about everybody in the camp was scared of loud noises. Aeroplanes sent most Syrians to the edge of a table or doorframe. Not quite crawling under, but ready to. The same thing happened when a jackhammer was brought in to break hard ground where the showers were being constructed.

But the biggest difference between us was shown to me one hot Thursday afternoon.

We walked through the camp, her in a Union Jack shirt and me in a singlet that showed my slowly tanning shoulders. Our feet crunched in the sand and dry dirt beneath us.

In some ways, I'd got used to the rows and rows of tents, and the faces that peeked out from them.

'When Grandma Teete got sick,' she said, 'I moved so I wouldn't be far from the hospital. It's much easier to move a tent than to move house.'

She stopped in front of a row of five tents – three nylon ones, a tiny Winnie the Pooh kid's tent and something that looked like a yurt.

'Which one's yours?'

She was biting the edge of her lip, 'This one,' and pointed to the little Winnie the Pooh tent.

The tent barely looked tall enough to kneel in. My eyes wandered over to the duct tape stretched like stitches over the tent's rips. Parts of it were faded from the sun. I swallowed and looked at Aya.

She didn't meet my eyes.

'You... stay here by yourself?' I asked.

'Me and grandma, but she doesn't need the tent at the moment so there's a little more space.'

I nodded, 'It's... nice Aya.'

'I wish you hadn't come.'

'Why?'

'Because look at it,' she turned to me, her voice was soft, 'It's a kid's tent, and we've been living in it two years. Teete got pneumonia because it leaks in winter.' She was breathing heavily. 'It sucks, but I'm used to it, I just hate you seeing it.'

I shook my head, 'I'm impressed. You know how to look after yourself.'

She stood watching me, arms by her sides. I reached out. I wanted to hug her. Instead, I just touched her shoulder. Her skin was warm.

'I haven't met anyone our age that's as strong as you are. You've done so well Aya.'

She gave a hearty sniff and wrapped her arms around me, I could feel her quick breaths through her chest, 'You're a great liar.'

She wiped her nose and laughed, stepping back from me, 'Do you want to see inside?'

'Yes!'

She unzipped the flaps and folded them back, then untangled her mosquito netting and spread out her hands... 'My humble castle.'

Inside, a large inflatable mattress took up most of the floor. A collection of sleeping bags and blankets sat on top of it. Beside the entrance, a gas cooker stood along with a small pan, pot, and two plates, two cups, and two bowls.

In the left corner was an iron-framed pack with a small sack of dried rice sitting on top.

'You need to see it at night sometime,' she touched a black battery box hanging from the tent roof. 'I found an old set of fairy lights in the trash and managed to twist the wires together to get them working again.'

She smiled as she flicked a small black switch, it looked like Winnie the Pooh was flying amongst the stars, 'Grandma was proud – they're like something you'd see on Pinterest.'

I turned to her, 'Wait... you know what Pinterest is?'

'Yeah,' she rolled her eyes, 'Although grandma used it more than I did. I also know Tumblr, Snapchat, Instagram, WhatsApp, WeChat, Facebook and all the other hundred million social medias. We lived in Syria, not the 1920s.'

'So, you have a phone?'

She climbed into the tent and ruffled around in the iron-framed backpack until she pulled out a solid looking touch-screen from a brand I didn't recognise.

'Only problem is I can't afford data or texts or anything and there's no wifi here. I just keep it charged for the day I start to travel again.'

'Then how do you keep in contact with your family?'

She froze halfway through putting her phone back in the bag, then slowly shook her head. 'I've depressed you enough already.'

I climbed into the tent behind her, and sat down on the air mattress, 'Yeah I get that. My family situation isn't the best either. Perhaps we can trade stories some time – some night?'

She nodded, 'Under the stars and the fairy lights.'

As Ayamin talked, I slowly became aware of how close we were, how we were together *alone*. I looked into her eyes and she smiled as she talked. I wondered if she was leaning closer to me. I was leaning closer to her. We were just an arm's length apart. *Within kissing distance*. Everything around her was blurring. Her lips were pink and red. They moved slowly as she spoke...

'Hello, Danny? What are you doing?'

Ayamin's voice pulled me back into the real world. She had an odd expression on her face. I blinked, then tried to grin. It felt forced.

'What was that?' I said, coughing to cover the fact that my face was turning red.

'I said tonight? You could be a thief, sneak out, and bring me ice cream. We can watch the stars and eat ice cream from the tub.'

I felt my grin returning, 'I'll find you your ice cream.'

She laughed, 'Great...' then she touched the side of my head, 'You okay?'

I tried to think of some way to make myself sound moody or mysterious, but in the end, I just had to shrug, 'It happens when I talk to beautiful girls.'

She laughed, 'Alright Augustus Waters. Go find me some ice cream – anything with berries in it is my favourite.'

****

It was midnight before I was sure everyone was asleep. At dinner we'd been warned again about the dangers of sneaking out. These included; death, being held hostage, broken bones, getting a cold, and no dessert for a month.

But at the same time, I didn't care. There was a beautiful girl waiting for her ice cream and I intended to deliver.

I veered off from the bathroom and made my way into the kitchen where I'd stored a spare ice cream carton in the top freezer. Ice cream was strictly for celebrations, but I figured any time I got to spend with Ayamin was a celebration.

I slid back the door and slipped outside, then crouched down beside the wall and waited for our guard to move off.

There was a slight chill in the air, almost enough to make me want something more than a t-shirt. I could hear a baby crying and vehicles on a faraway road.

The soldier moved to the other side of the containers. The hollow thud of his boots disappeared. I ran.

The night air cooled me. All the tents were various shades of grey. It was only the starry sky that had any colour to it.

I made it to the hospital and retraced the route Ayamin had shown me. I reached the Winnie the Pooh tent and stopped, listening to see if she was awake.

A zip sounded and Ayamin's head popped out, 'About time. I could hardly sleep.'

She grabbed my hand and pulled me inside, boots and all. Ayamin zipped up the tent and turned to me, a flashlight was in one hand, and her face deadly serious.

'Please tell me you brought ice cream.'

I almost joked that we had none left, but I realised she'd tear me apart before I could say I was kidding. I handed the carton over.

Her voice cracked as she spoke, 'I didn't actually... expect you to have it.' She held the ice cream like a child as she gazed at it, 'Boysenberry, oh man.'

She threw her arms around me, tackling me onto the airbed.

'Ayamin,' I laughed, 'Are you crying?'

'I really miss ice cream,' she held me a moment longer, her head was warm against my chest. 'Now let's get some tea-spoons and we can watch these stars.'

While I ruffled through her kitchen box Ayamin went out-side and there was a zipping sound. She tugged at the tent until I could see a square patch of the stars above us. She crawled into the tent beside me. I handed her the ice cream and a spoon and we lay back on the inflatable mattress, looking up at the sky.

My eyes adjusted until the stars glowed bright. I could see red, white, orange, and purple.

'If we were more practical grandma and I could have found a slightly better tent. But if we weren't able to see the sky when-ever we wanted, I don't think we'd have made it this far.'

She pulled out a spoonful of vanilla ice cream with boy-senberries dripping from it, put the spoon in her mouth and closed her eyes.

A moan came from her throat. Ayamin shook her head, 'Six months of care packages and a sack of rice. You have no idea how good this taste.'

I tried to imagine that I was in her position, nothing but bland food for months... probably some of them spent on the brink of starvation. I touched the spoon to my lips and closed my eyes.

It was okay, probably on par with the cheapest stuff you could buy in supermarkets, but Ayamin didn't seem to care. She treated the ice cream like it was made of gold.

'When I move to Britain,' she said, 'I'm going to eat ice cream after dinner every night. I'm going to become an ice cream collector; I'll make world records for the amount of ice cream I eat.'

She took another spoonful and handed the tub back to me, 'When I'm sad I'll have special ice cream for that. When I'm happy I'll have ice cream to celebrate.'

Her words made my next mouthful sweeter – I could taste the boysenberries, the cream.

'Where in Britain would you go?'

She shifted slightly on the mattress. Her arm came to rest against mine.

'Well, I'd live in London to start with. I want to feel what it's like to live there, see the snow on the streets in winter, get a hot chocolate, and listen to people complain about the weather. I want to ride the underground and the London Eye and find a hidden bookshop in the backstreets.'

'Then maybe the Scottish Highlands, a little cottage to make all cosy, all the beautiful lochs and old stone buildings you could ask for. After that who knows? Maybe Ireland, Wales...'

She was silent for a moment, 'That's the dream anyway. I'm still a long way from England, but when there's no boysenberry ice cream on standby a dream can be the only thing to get you through.'

We stared up at the stars. Her arm against me was warm. I coughed and shifted a little closer.

'You can come visit me, wherever the hell I'm living when I get back.'

Ayamin smiled up at me, 'I'd like that. Maybe you can show me around. Take me to your parents.'

'Umm...I could show you around... definitely.'

When I looked at Ayamin her eyes had this softness to them and her voice was low, 'I forgot – tough family situation – I'm sorry.'

There was a moment of silence. When I spoke my voice was low and cracked, 'I'm a foster care freak. Biologically speaking the people who created me are still walking around going about their lives. I just never met them.'

Her hand brushed my hand, then her fingers found the gaps between my fingers, 'That's rough Danny.'

I could see this epic swirl from the milky way, 'How about you?'

'I think I was kinda lucky, loving mum and dad, annoying little brother, and my grandma lived with us so I almost had two mums. It was a perfect little setup until about two years ago when an artillery shell or... something, blew up our house.'

She gave a little gasp, 'Grandma and I were out buying bread. The house was basically dust, and we never even saw their bodies. After that we walked across the border, found a tent and shared it until her pneumonia got too bad.'

Her hand squeezed mine, 'I feel like your story is worse in some ways, you never even got to know them.'

I rubbed her thumb, 'I don't feel the pain you do, it's sort of a distant longing.'

We stopped talking for a while and I listened to the sound of Ayamin breathing. The air was starting to get a little chilly, but the places where our arms touched were just fine.

'I've never had a conversation like this in English,' Ayamin turned to look at me.

I laughed, 'I'm available any time.'

She pulled a large woollen blanket from the front of the tent and draped it over the two of us, then leaned back, resting her head on my chest. She yawned as I put an arm around her.

If this was any other girl in any other place, I would've made my next move right then. Maybe a kiss on the forehead, or a not-so-subtle caress. But this felt different.

Maybe it was because we'd opened up to each other, or because I wasn't even sure whether she liked me that way. Either way, I figured it wasn't worth losing the beautiful Syrian girl.

I stared up at the sky and felt the slow rising and falling of her breath against my side. She was warm and it made me sleepy and comfortable just having her there.

****

As summer began to rear its head my Arabic began to improve. It was a weird feeling. I'd never done well in school, was never good at learning, but I guess having a hot teacher helped.

When I could speak 'as well as a four-year-old' Ayamin dragged me to the hospital and stood me in front of Grandma Teete.

'Teete,' I said, 'Yo'borneh jamelik.'

The old woman gave a delighted snort of laughter, then coughed, then clapped her hands and said three words in Arabic over and over.

Ayamin's face went red.

'I don't know that one,' I said to Ayamin, 'What does it mean?'

She shook her head, 'It was a joke.' Teete laughed even harder.

'Can you translate it?'

But she wouldn't. Instead, she picked up her novel, and held it close to her face so it covered her cheeks, 'We're almost through *Two Hearts in the French Night*, I thought maybe we could do an extra reading session today.' When I looked at Teete, the old woman winked.

Ayamin read, and as she did the brightness on her cheeks calmed down.

'I don't think I've ever been this happy,' Rudy told her.

'I know... there's something special about this town.'

Rudy shook his head, his thumb moved to Samantha's cheek, 'There's something special about you.'

After she'd read two chapters, Ayamin closed the book and looked from Teete to me.

'Do you want to come over for some tea?' she asked without looking at me.

I looked around to see if the hospital staff were watching. I still had two hours left in the day, but as far as I could tell there were no messages that needed delivering.

'Let's do it.'

She gave her grandma a kiss on the cheek and flicked her head, 'Come on Danny-boy.'

I said goodbye to Teete in Arabic and watched her laugh, she had the sort of laugh that doesn't hold back, loud and proud, only once again her laugh turned into a cough, she pulled tissues from the box beside her and coughed into them. Little drops of red began to soak through. She tried to throw the used tissues into a plastic white bin beside her bed, but they bounced out. The bin already had a small mountain of tissues inside of it. Each of the crumpled white sheets of paper had the same bright red stain on them.

****

Ayamin was quiet as we walked through the camp. Her air mattress sat on the sand outside the Winnie the Pooh tent and she rubbed her eyes as we sat on it, looking out at the refugees. There was laughing and the pounding of feet as kids chased each other through the tents. A woman began to cook a pot of rice. I breathed in; the camp had a faint rotten garbage smell.

'I'm sorry Danny.'

'What for?'

Ayamin was looking down at her feet, 'For not being fun today. It hurts when she hurts.'

'It's okay,' I reached down and slipped my hand under hers, Aya's fingers curled between mine and then she dug her toes into the sandy dirt.

'It's just... I want her life to be more than a hospital bed.' she paused for a moment and stared up at the sky, 'How would you feel about taking her on a mission to see the stars?'

'Teete? Tonight?'

'Tonight.'

I grinned a big toothy grin, and that was all the answer she needed, she pushed my shoulder, 'You're too much Danny.'

****

I didn't realise how good I was getting at sneaking out until I was past our guard and running towards Ayamin's tent.

It was closing in on midnight – most of the camp was in bed, but there were still refugees who peered from tents as I ran past.

Winnie the Pooh's face was lit by the gas cooker Ayamin used to boil water. Beside her sat two plastic cups and a bowl. She hugged me the moment I was in reach.

'I'm glad we're doing this tonight,' she poured the steaming water into her bowl and added tea leaves. 'She's getting tired.'

We carried our tea through the camp. The air hardly had a chill to it and we wore just a single layer each.

At night the makeshift hospital was probably the nosiest place in the camp. As we slipped into it someone was crying out for a family member. Ayamin paused as we passed them. She turned to me and whispered.

'They're dreaming about home.'

'Really?' One man was shrieking like he'd been stabbed, three beds down from him a little girl was curled up in a ball whimpering. A wet stain showed through her blanket.

'It sounds more like nightmares to me.'

Ayamin just nodded, 'That is home for us.'

As we walked a few patients looked up, but no one spoke to us. We made it through to Grandma Teete who lay on her back, breathing deep. A pale light made the wrinkles around her eyes stand out. Ayamin placed the tea on the table beside her.

'Teete.' she said, 'Teete?'

Grandma Teete rubbed her eyes and looked up, she had a childlike smile on her face, 'Aya?'

Then she began to cough, long and hard. Aya fetched tissue from the table beside her and helped Teete clean the blood from her hands.

Teete croaked a few words into Ayamin's ear and Ayamin told her about the night sky.

'Aya – aya.'

We slid the locks off her bed and gently pushed it down the hallway. Grandma Teete was doing her best not to giggle, occasionally a tiny bit of laughter would escape her and Ayamin would hold her finger to her lips. When I laughed Ayamin rolled her eyes, 'The two of you would make very bad secret agents.'

The patients who couldn't sleep stared at us, one guy called out, but nobody stopped us. We moved through the hospital to the entrance and pushed Teete into the night sky.

We set up camp slightly away from the hospital, jacking up Grandma Teete's bed so she could drink her tea.

The stars were a blanket of light and dark above us. Stripes and shades of blue were mixed between them in a slowly moving dance. The night's chill was sweet like dew, and Teete sang a happy-sad song that only we could hear.

Her music died out, and we stood, gazing into the abyss of everything that exists. I felt small, and at the same time just right. A warm hand slipped into mine.

There was a cough, and then another. I tore my eyes away from the stars to Teete, her face strained as she coughed, and her hands held her chest.

Ayamin and I looked at each other, we took a side of her bed each and began wheeling her back in.

Teete's hands found our wrists and she squeezed them while we passed through the white hospital doors. As we put the locks back on her bed a light coming from some of the equipment showed the tears running down her face.

She spoke four soft words in Arabic, and Ayamin started to cry.

I looked at her, 'What does it mean?'

Ayamin opened her mouth, but her voice didn't seem to work, I laid a hand on her shoulder as she sobbed, she wiped her eyes and whispered to me.

'It means I love you... it means thank you.'

Teete took my hand, she took Ayamin's, she held them together between hers and repeated the words.

The old lady burst into another coughing fit and I felt my eyes water. Ayamin looked at me, tears streaming down her face.

The sound of footsteps came from the end of the hallway. A white nurse's uniform moved through the patients. They stopped to check on someone.

We squeezed Grandma Teete's hands, she nodded, and we ran.

I pushed through the hospital's flap doors. The outside felt colder without hot tea and Grandma Teete. Ayamin pulled me into a hug.

'You did good Aya,' I said, rubbing her back, 'I'll see you tomorrow?'

I tried to step back but Ayamin's feet dragged on the ground, her arms were still around me, 'Come with me, I won't sleep alone.'

I glanced back toward the barracks; I would have to slip back in at some point. Then I saw the tears on her face and touched my thumb to her cheek.

'I can't stay long.'

I held her, then lifted her, and carried her back to the tent.

'I'm such a sook,' she said as she rocked against me, 'It's just she's the only one left. When Teete goes it'll just be me. Alone.'

I didn't know what to say and I didn't know how to say it. Her cheek brushed mine. She'd been strong, but the world had been brutal. I wanted to protect her.

Ayamin let out another sob as we unzipped the tent and crawled inside. She pushed off her shoes, and pulled a blanket over her, leaving the left side of the inflatable mattress uncovered.

I lay down beside her. Ayamin reached around me with the blanket until I was part of her cocoon. She curled up with her back against my chest. Her hair tickled my nose.

'You have no idea how happy she was to see those stars,' she said.

'I could see her smile.'

Ayamin's hands found my arm and held it to her, 'That little song she sang when she was looking at the sky – it was about people flying amongst the stars.'

I breathed in the warm air between us, 'Tomorrow let's look for a Teete Star, she can pick any one she wants.'

Ayamin was quiet for a minute, I felt her chest rising and falling and the beating of her heart, 'Thanks Danny,' she said.

'For what?'

'For being here, for being you.'

I lay there another two hours, staring at the roof of the tent. Ayamin passed out, but I knew I wouldn't sleep.

Then, as the sky began to tinge red, I slipped out from next to her and ran back to the container.

****

I managed half an hour of sleep before our wake-up call sounded. My eyes were hooded and I truly felt that I was a zombie waking from the dead.

The rest of the juvies talked amongst themselves. I don't think they even looked at me. I just inhaled my wheat biscuits and tossed my bowl into the sink.

Breathing in the cool morning air I walked down to the hospital. I was excited and a little scared about last night. *I'm pretty sure she's into me.* I walked through the hospital tents, whistled a little, then stopped.

In front of Grandma Teete's bed there were four people. A doctor, two nurses, and Ayamin.

The way the doctor was shaking his head as he chatted to the nurses and the way Ayamin was holding Teete's poppy while a nurse rubbed her back told me everything I needed to know.

I walked a little closer to the bed. Teete's face was blue, her eyes were shut, and her chest didn't move.

I felt Ayamin's arms around me. She was crying and touched her forehead to my chest. The doctor narrowed his eyes, but I didn't care. I wrapped my arms around her.

'Hey, hey,' I said, rubbing circles in her back the way I'd seen one of my foster Mums do. 'She went happy.'

Ayamin nodded and looked up at me, tears streaked her face, and her hair was a mess, but there was something in her eyes. As the doctor and nurses moved away, Ayamin whispered to me.

'I'm alone.'

I looked back at Grandma Teete and felt tears begin to well up.

'I'm here,' I promised.

She nodded like she didn't believe me, and then turned back to Teete. We took seats to the side of her.

'I'm done with this camp. I'm going to head for Britain,' Her hands traced the route on an invisible map as she listed the journey through Turkey and the boat trip to Greece, 'I've heard plenty of talk about what route is best.'

'You're serious about this?'

Her hands fell to her sides, 'There's no future for me here.'

'But you shouldn't go alone. It's dangerous.'

She rolled her eyes, 'A bomb hit my house Danny, and I was out buying bread. By rights, I shouldn't even be here. If I'm dead, what can hurt me?'

Her eyes were drying and she seemed to have a new spirit in her. But it was a dangerous spirit. 'I've got a lot to do.' She took a shaky breath and her tears began to flow again, 'And then there's Teete.'

Ayamin had nothing to pay for Grandma Teete's funeral, so there wasn't much of a ceremony. A line of holes had been pre-prepared and within an hour we were covering her body with dirt.

Ayamin dropped the last shovelful of crumbling dirt onto the grave and rested on her shovel, staring down at the grave and its simple white marker.

'She wanted me to go,' Ayamin said, 'She didn't like me staying here and wasting my life. But I'm glad I did.'

'She always told me to make sure I visit Paris,' Ayamin pulled out her copy of *Two Hearts in the French Night* and placed Teete's poppy inside of it.

Then Ayamin turned away from the grave and looked out beyond the camp entrance.

****

I fought with my eyes and the dark to stay awake. The nights of lost sleep were catching up with me. Still. I had to visit Ayamin. I pushed myself from under the covers and rolled until I was sitting on the floor of the container.

A glance at my nearly dead iPhone showed that it was midnight, time to take my chances. I threw the phone into my pocket, pulled on a woollen jersey, then stared at my boots.

Do I need them? I'm not going far. I shrugged and laced them up anyway, they'd be a little clunky, but keep my feet clean for Ayamin's tent.

My boots seemed extra loud as I made my way into the kitchen.

The door was locked, probably thanks to me, so I jimmied up the window and slipped out into the night.

Running so our guard wouldn't see me, I made my way down an avenue of tents to where I knew the Winnie the Pooh mansion was.

The only trouble is, the tent wasn't there. I took a couple of steps backwards and looked toward the hospital, trying to reorient myself. I stared at the outlines of the two tents nearby – one looked like a yurt, the other was a dome nylon tent. They were the same.

It was only when I crouched that I saw the flat rectangle from where her tent used to be. That was it. She'd gone.

I stood up like I had arthritis. Slowly and in pain. I couldn't breathe properly.

'AYAMIN.' I yelled, forgetting I was surrounded by sleeping people. Someone in a tent to my right yelled 'shut up,' in Arabic.

I realised no one else gave a damn about the poor Syrian girl who'd left here on her own.

My fists hit the ground over and over again, I needed some physical escape to get me away from my thoughts. *Why did I sleep so long?*

I stood up, fists burning, and started to run. The entrance to the camp stood in front of me, but as I ran towards it, I saw the silhouette of two guards talking to each other.

I turned left and found the spot where the fence didn't quite reach the ground. I slipped through the hole and was up and running again, my stiff legs relaxed with each step.

Initially, I simply wanted to outrun my thoughts and with a constant *slap, slap,* on the tarmac I did. But as my legs began to tire, I realised I'd met a road that was headed north – the same way Ayamin would have travelled.

I kept running. My body got hot under the woollen sweater I'd thrown on. Without stopping I slipped it over my head and tied it around my neck where it bounced with each step.

Occasionally a vehicle would flash by, ruining my night vision.

My thighs began to feel like mud, my calf muscles tightened up, and eventually I was forced to slow a jog. The slower pace gave me time to think which wasn't necessarily a good thing. I realised there were dozens of roads heading north, and that even if she had taken this one Ayamin would've hidden to one of the sides if she heard a heffalump like me pounding along the road behind her.

I slowed to a walk. All the energy and shock had gone from mc. Ayamin was gone.

There was a smooth boulder on the side of the road. I stared at its silhouette for a moment before I sat on it and pulled my legs up to my chest. I thought back on my time with Ayamin and tried to convince myself that just the memories of her would be enough.

By the time I had to pull my woollen jersey back on, I knew the memories would never be enough. I wanted to make more memories with Ayamin. I wanted *her*.

I lept from the rock. The ground was softer here, but the skin of my fist still tore as it thumped against the earth. I only stopped hitting the ground when blood ran down my hand.

As I sat there panting, I noticed a satellite bobbing up and down just above the road from where I'd come from.

It moved closer and gained in size and became brighter than a satellite. The sound of footsteps reached me and I watched, mouth gaping, as Ayamin walked past me.

I jumped up from my rock and ran towards her, 'Ayamin!' I yelled, 'Ayamin!'

'What??' Ayamin shouted back, a scowl on her face.

'I wanted to see you.'

'Well,' she said, 'Here I am.' she turned away, 'And I have a long walk ahead of me.'

I walked beside her as she set off down the road again. The crunch of her footsteps seemed loud in the night.

'Where are you going?'

'England.'

'And you're walking there on your own? With only Winnie the Pooh for shelter?'

Her eyes narrowed at me, 'It's enough. It's what I've got.'

Ayamin stopped walking. I stopped walking. She wobbled and leaned into me. In the starlight, I could see tears forming in her lashes.

'Look at me,' she wiped at her eyes, 'Only a couple of kilometres down the road and I'm already starting to cry.'

She shook her head, 'Do you think I'll make it Danny?'

I wrapped my arms around her, helping to support the large backpack that hung behind her, 'With your spirit, I think you will... in fact I know you will.'

She looked up and tested a smile. In the starry night she looked beautiful, 'How do you know?'

'Because I'm coming with you.'

The words tumbled from my mouth before my brain had a chance to consider them, but I knew they were as true as the earth. I couldn't abandon Ayamin, something about her just wouldn't let me.

Although, clearly she didn't feel the same way.

Ayamin pushed my chest, throwing herself out of our hug and pointed her finger at me, 'Don't talk stupid Danny.'

I held my hands up, 'What? You expect me to stay?'

'Of course I do, you have a ride home to Britain and a place to stay when you get there and all those people back at the camp, they'll miss you if you just disappear.'

'I don't care. It wouldn't be right to let you go alone.'

Ayamin sighed and put her face in her hands. Then she turned and started walking north. 'Go home Danny.'

I followed along about ten meters behind, my hands in my pockets.

Ayamin tried to speed up her pace, but with the big backpack on her shoulders I kept up easily. She tried to go down false roads and double back but I just waited for her. She even tried throwing rocks at me, but she wasn't exactly a born cricketer and they bounced near my feet.

'Go away!'

'No.'

She spun, fists clenched, 'You want me to throw more rocks?'

I held a hand to my chin, and thought about it a moment, 'Actually, yes.'

'Why?'

'Because it's funny.'

Her hand shot to the ground, picked up a rock, and swung it in my direction. With a soft *thwack*, the stone landed two metres to my right.

I laughed.

'You moved,' Ayamin yelled.

'I did not.'

'Well... you look like a fish.'

'What sort of fish?'

'An ugly fish.'

That made me laugh. She spun around again and I hid my grin, 'Ayamin, you look like a princess.'

She snorted and tried to speed up her footsteps, 'What sort of princess?'

'An ugly princess.'

For a moment she laughed, then she tried to hide it with a cough.

'I'd rather be an ugly princess than an ugly fish.'

The two of us walked and yelled insults and told bad jokes about each other until the sun came up. It was bright red, and although I hadn't slept, the cool air and the sun's magic revived me.

We hit the city of Izmir just as the morning traffic started to get bad. The honks and angry Turkish shouts were a far cry from the stillness of the country roads we'd walked on. Back then the only shouting came from us.

As we got into the city proper and the smell of cars became our every breath Ayamin stopped running forwards when I walked next to her. She appeared to accept that I was coming along but still wouldn't give me anything more than one-word answers.

'Which smugglers are we going to?' I asked.

'Any.'

'How do we know they're trustworthy?'

'We don't.'

'What will we do if they rip us off?'

'Nothing.'

'Are you still angry?'

'Yes.'

We made our way through the city. It was only as Ayamin stopped for lunch that my rumbling stomach reminded me of how ill-prepared I was.

Aside from my woollen sweater and walking boots I had a pair of shorts, my t-shirt, and a nearly-dead iPhone. I didn't have any way of withdrawing the money I had in England.

I watched as Ayamin counted and recounted her coins, she was staring at a small loaf of Turkish bread in a baker's stall. She glanced at me and sighed, adding a few more coins to the pile in her left hand.

She walked up to the stall and pointed to the Turkish loaf, handing over the coins. The baker pulled the loaf from the shelf, put it in a brown paper bag, and with a nod, handed it to her.

Ayamin turned, snapped her bread in half and gave the larger part to me.

'Thanks.' I mumbled, feeling like a complete burden.

But the bread was soft, with spices that made my mouth water when I bit into it. I wolfed down most of the loaf before we'd left the shop.

We passed through a market on our way to the sea. Yellow, red, and deep ochre spices lured my nose and eyes through it. There was this constant noise of people bartering and comparing and begging in different languages and it all felt so much more alive than the camp had.

We reached the edge of the market and the beginning of the Aegean Sea. Small waves lapped up against the harbour. We watched as a cruise ship filled with British and Americans set sail. Some of the people on board looked almost... *bored.*

Ayamin touched my arm, then pointed to a couple standing on the harbour. They wore tattered clothes, and at their feet sat two large backpacks. Like us, they'd been watching the ship.

'They're Syrian too,' she said and walked towards them with her arms outstretched. Ayamin began speaking to them, the two looked from her to me and back again. The guy in particular looked wary when he saw me.

Ayamin asked something and the man pointed out a route through the streets with his finger. Ayamin nodded and gave a mini bow. Then the four of us parted ways.

'They told me where I can find a smuggler,' she said, 'He'll take me to Greece, I can make my way from there.'

'Don't you mean we?'

'If you cross this sea Danny that's it, there's no going back.' Her warm hand touched my chest, 'You're a brave and stupid and amazing boy. But this isn't your world.'

I looked back, the two Syrians were still watching me. I thought about not being able to speak Arabic, *Maybe she's right? I don't know this place.*

I was about to turn around. To admit that I was way out of my depth.

But then I watched her struggle to lift the pack onto her shoulders. I could see rainclouds out at sea. I thought about what I was going back to. *A camp without Ayamin. No home back in England. Three convictions to my name.*

'My life is shit,' I pulled the iPhone from my pocket, 'I've got the money for my ticket right here.'

She shook her head and stormed off towards the sea.

I got a stack of money for my iPhone from some guy who didn't speak English, but gave me the biggest handshake in the world when I traded with him.

I was feeling pretty good about the deal until Ayamin saw the stack of notes in my hand.

'You idiot!' she said. 'That'll barely be enough for a ticket. You could've got twice that.' She threw her hands up, 'But I'm not talking to you so it's not my problem.'

Within minutes nearly all my money was in the hands of one of the smugglers. The guy had greasy hair and a shark's grin. He passed us a lifejacket each and led us into a concrete shed to wait.

Inside there were people hunched up on sagging white benches. A strong scent of vomit mixed with bleach and seawater filled the air. We found ourselves a section of bench and sat.

Next to me, Ayamin shivered slightly. She leaned her head back against the damp wall.

****

'BOAT,' came the cry in Arabic.

Ayamin and I sat up at the same time. The sun was down and the smuggler with greasy hair was walking through the shed, whispering for us to get ready and banging a hollow steel pipe on the floor. He grabbed a woman in his way and shoved her in the direction of the boat ramp.

Ayamin's skin was pale. Her lips shook as she breathed in.

We stood up. Ayamin placed her phone, book, and money into plastic bags. Then I took the pack and slipped it onto my back.

Across from us two ladies were crying. They had a young girl with them who started bawling too. The smuggler came over and pushed a rag into the kid's face. He grabbed the woman's arm and slapped it over thc rag. Thc kid cried even harder.

'When outside keep it quiet,' the smuggler growled in Arabic.

There were shouts ahead of us as we moved towards the boat. We rounded a concrete wall and saw our ship. It was an orange inflatable lifeboat with sagging sides and bits of canvas peeling off it. The people closest to the boat had stopped moving. Their feet were turning around as their confidence plummeted.

The smugglers grabbed people's luggage and threw it on. They were laughing.

'No refunds. Noooo reeeefunds.'

We moved a step closer in the line that had formed. I looked around. The boat was made for twenty people. Around us there were fifty.

As I took my seat on the sagging orange canvas I wondered briefly if they had a second boat. I doubted it.

When I looked out, I saw three men standing with arms crossed over their chests. One was arguing with a smuggler. Their families, weighed down by large bags, stood behind them. The kids were crying.

As the boat filled up, I watched the men's heads drop and they allowed the smugglers to guide them on board.

Ayamin's hands travelled up my arm. She took deep breaths.

I stared out towards the dark sea. Felt the water rock the boat beneath our feet.

The smugglers were fast. Fifty of us were packed like sardines returning to the sea. The two who'd helped load the ship hopped off and the greasy-haired smuggler started up his engine.

We moved into the harbour; our boat sat dangerously low in the dark water. Suddenly light flooded into the boat as a large cruise ship passed through. The smuggler called out in Arabic and parents around us wrapped their hands around their children's mouths. Trying to stifle their sobs.

The muted crying made the water's slap deafening as it hit the side of our boat. The cruise ship's wake rocked us from side to side and the light was blinding.

With a large swoosh of water, the ship moved away from us and the smuggler started our engine again. A tinny rattling sound moved through the boat as we sped from the harbour.

Right at the edge a small motorboat sat waiting.

'It's the police.' a refugee in front of me said, 'No,' someone else whispered, 'It's just more smugglers.'

I wasn't sure which option I preferred.

The motorboat carried a blinding light that made me turn my head away. Ayamin held her hands in front of her eyes. Her hair was blowing everywhere.

The greasy smuggler handed the control of the engine to the refugee next to him.

Then the smuggler stood up, took two steps and jumped into the motorboat. He yelled to the man steering it who swung the boat around with a great churn of water and headed back into the harbour.

Everyone watched the small boat disappear. Apart from the waves swishing around us, and the howl of the wind, there was silence. We were alone.

A baby began to cry and then another one. They broke our collective trance, and everyone turned to the refugee who'd been given control of the motor.

He looked to be in his mid-twenties and sat alone. His eyes, full of worry, swept the boat until they landed on a little baby girl wrapped up in a pink blanket. The girl was quiet. Watching the world with an aged interest.

The young man at the engine wrapped his fingers tight around the steering bar. Our engine spluttered to life, and the boat began to move once more.

The moment we passed the breakwater big rolling black waves lifted us and dumped us back down. I could hear a child screaming. Ayamin squeezed off the side of the boat to hold a little boy in her arms. She was crying. But then again, we all were.

I wrapped one arm around her and the kid, my other arm clung to the boat.

A wave hit our side and cold salty water flew up and coated us. A shock went through my body and for a few seconds, I forgot how to breathe. The kid squirmed in Ayamin's arms and cried harder.

Half a plastic soft drink bottle hit my head. I looked up to see the man next to me grab it and use it to bail out the water that was soaking into our shoes.

Two scoops later and another wave reared up and hit us from the other side. Around the boat, the refugees began scooping in earnest. I used my free hand, but I only managed three scoops before the next wave rained down on us.

The steady drone of the little motor began to be drowned out by the wails coming from around us. Ayamin squeezed the little boy but it didn't help. His screams pierced my ears. *Crash.* Another wave filled the boat.

'For what it's worth.' Ayamin said, her saturated clothes shivering, 'I'm really glad you're with me.'

I nodded. My breath was foggy.

She leaned forward and pressed her forehead against mine. Another wave hit us and her head moved to my shoulder.

'I'm so scared Danny.'

I shifted my arm around her back. Moved it in circles as I fought back sobs.

In the distance, I saw a mountain rising out of the sea. Only the mountain was moving closer to us.

It travelled to us in slow motion. Nobody else seemed to be looking, everyone was coughing or bailing water.

By the time the young man who was steering realised what was coming it was too late. The mountain-wave fell, half breaking over the boat, and slamming hundreds of litres of water into it. The refugees scooped. But not enough.

The next wave didn't lift us up, it tilted us until we were vertical. People scrambled over each other and children got crushed. The angle of the boat passed ninety degrees and it flipped.

We plunged five meters into the water, the cold impact slammed the air out of me. I tried to get a gulp of air. Someone's legs kicked at me. When I swam to the side my head hit the boat.

It was dark and the water swirled above us. My eyes stung from the salt. I kicked my legs in one direction until I couldn't swim any more. Popping up to the surface. I tasted the air just as a wave passed over me.

I surfaced again and coughed up the water I'd swallowed. The cold was getting into my bones. I looked at the boat and all the refugees trying to right it.

It was hopeless. As the waves pounded past, I looked for Ayamin. I couldn't see her.

I swam towards a cluster of people. The waves lifted and dropped us. I spotted black hair and called out.

'Ayamin!'

'Danny?!'

I paddled to her and reached out with a shaking arm until my forehead touched hers. Another wave crashed next to us. She took a deep breath.

'I don't want to die today.'

'We've just got to keep afloat. Keep warm.'

We stayed close to each other. The refugees had given up on righting the boat and were pushing the children onto the hull. More waves buckled the boat, but the people holding onto it in the water kept it flat.

We swam with tired arms until we found the boat. Holding onto the edges side by side. I put my hand on hers. There was no warmth in her fingers. I decided I wasn't going to let go of her hand – I didn't fear the cold or the currents – only letting go.

'I'm sorry I got you into this Danny.'

'I'm not. It was t-too hot in Turkey anyway.'

She cry-laughed a little. Her arms shivered and her clothes were stuck to her body. Ayamin went to speak but was cut short as a ship's horn tore through the air. We looked up and a flashlight settled on our overturned boat. Then another. They were blinding after being in the dark for so long.

A ship cut through the water towards us, a white and blue Greek flag was painted on its side.

I saw Ayamin's face had gone dark purple.

'Yes! YES! Over here! Damn yes!'

All the refugees who'd crowded around the lifeboat were yelling, calling for the boat. It was a cacophony of noise.

There were two ladders on the side closest to us, and the refugees began swimming to them. Climbing up the ladder like drowned rats.

Ayamin reached it and with shaking arms heaved herself up the side of the boat. I followed, my hands aching as they took me up the ladder. At the top, someone from the crew hauled us on, pointed to spots on the wet deck, and yelled at us to sit.

One by one the Syrians were loaded on. One man was carrying his kid and crying. The crew from the boat pulled the kid away from him and started pumping his chest. Every few beats they'd pause and blow air into the child's lungs.

More people came on board and we shifted to a spot near the railings. The wind there blew cold and wet, but we weren't about to die. Ayamin nestled herself against me and we watched as the crew gave their last attempt to save the little boy.

'That's the one I held,' she whispered with trembling lips, 'He looked like my brother.'

One of the boat people stepped aside to let the captain look at the boy. The captain gazed from the boy to the sea and shouted something in Greek.

He bent down and pumped the boy's chest with his hands, a fast motion, then breathed into the boy's mouth. He did it again, almost violently. The father was screaming at him. Then the boy coughed. He turned on his side and threw up a mouthful of water.

The crew let the boy's dad go and he bent down to touch his son's cheek. He was passed a blanket which he gently wrapped the boy in. One of the boat people knelt and helped him.

The man stood and hugged the captain. Light from the cabin illuminated tears as they mixed with the seawater on the men's skin.

****

We were unloaded at the ship's home in Paralia Kimis, Greece. Our army of refugees filed into the coastguard building looking like drowned rats, but feeling like we'd just escaped a mousetrap. In the kitchen, three Greek women were boiling massive pots of tea, hot chocolate, and coffee.

Ayamin sniffed the air, 'Oh my,' she said, 'Hot chocolate!!'

She grabbed my hand and yanked me to the line. In front of us was a steaming, frothing mass of bliss. Aya and I took a hot cup in each hand. We sat in a corner of the kitchen looking out at tired refugees warming themselves in front of heaters. Some dried their hair with towels, couples and families huddled under large woollen blankets.

I turned to Ayamin, the lights of the kitchen flickered a soft orange and yellow on her skin like the light of a campfire. She took a sip of hot chocolate and smiled a little smile of contentment. That's when I asked:

'Where next?'

Ayamin rolled her eyes, 'We just about drowned and already you're rearing for more.'

I took her hand, and rubbed my thumb along the back of it, her skin was still cold from the sea.

'Sorry... I just can't wait to get to England. Fish and chips and pork pie would be heaven right now.'

'Pork pie? Sounds... kinda gross, but I'll take your word for it?'

'Trust me, nothing can beat a steaming pork pie when you're cold. It gives you that cosy fulfilled feeling.'

We sat in comfortable, worn-out silence for a few minutes. Ayamin leant her head on my shoulder.

The refugee who'd been steering our boat limped over and crouched down beside us.

'The captain says everyone should get changed, it's not good to stay in wet clothes.'

I shrugged, looked down at my wet outfit, 'This is all we've got. Our bag was taken by the sea.'

'There's a place to get dry over there,' he said, pointing to a row of heaters, 'It's not good to stay in your wet clothes.'

'Thanks,' Ayamin said as he turned to relay the message to a family, 'You did a good job, to get us that far.'

He turned and held up two fingers next to his red eyes, 'Two people don't think so.'

'What did they say?' I said, 'You did the best you could. It's not your fault the smugglers abandoned us.'

The young man shook his head, 'They didn't say a thing. We left with fifty, there are forty-eight trying to get warm.'

He turned from us to the family. Ayamin's fingertips gripped my hand.

'Let's go warm up.'

****

As the night ended so did our stay at the coastguard clubrooms. A blaring alarm sounded and the crew came in, throwing on their life jackets and jumping into the boat.

The town's barber, probably one of the few residents who could speak Arabic, came out and asked us to leave.

'They go out to bring another boatload in. This town is not big enough,' the small wiry man said.

'But where do we go?' A woman asked. She had a kid holding each hand and her eyes were black rims.

The barber shrugged, 'Go north, or back, that's where everyone else went.'

He walked off and I looked at Ayamin, she also had the dark rings of insomnia. We all did. But her dark, wavy hair was tied back, she had her boots on, and a focussed look about her.

'Let's go,' she said.

Rays of sun peeked over the horizon as we started to walk, following the stream of refugees. We passed cafes and a waterfront market populated by foreign couples and families on vacation.

I waved to a man wearing a big Union Jack across his chest. He looked at me but must've been distracted. He didn't wave back.

'What are we going to do about a tent?' I asked, 'Oh, and more importantly, food.'

'Well I've got this,' she said, pulling a travel wallet from around her neck, she thumbed through her bills, then zipped it back up, 'We don't have anything for accommodation so we'll just have to rough it okay? And maybe go with a meal or two a day.'

She gave me a shove when she saw my face droop.

'Come on Danny, people *pay* to go on diets like this.'

'I know,' I grumbled half-heartedly. Inside I was feeling bad – but not because I might miss out on a couple of meals. I was reminded again that if I hadn't come Ayamin would have more money to spend on herself. I hadn't added anything to the expedition so far. I was basically a walking stomach.

You're going to have to become a working walking stomach, I thought to myself. *If we run out of money you need to provide Danny.*

My train of thought was interrupted by a call from behind us.

'Hey! Hey!'

We turned to see the refugee who'd been steering the boat running towards us. With a heave he dumped Ayamin's waterlogged hiking pack on the ground and looked up with a grin.

'They found it. The crew thought it was a person and fished it out of the water.'

Ayamin and I looked at each other. The bag was warmth, shelter, a way of carrying food. Big things when you've got nothing but the clothes on your back.

The two of us stepped over the bag and wrapped our arms around him.

'Thank you, thank you so much,' Ayamin said. When we stepped back, he was still grinning, 'I hope you make it to England.'

And then he was off again, running back down towards the coastguard.

'I don't know his name,' Ayamin said.

We turned to the bag; water leaked from it onto the roadside. She laughed, 'The universe is smiling on us.'

It took a little while to get the bag on my back, the water had more than doubled its weight, but Ayamin was keen to keep moving.

'Is it heavy?' she asked.

'No... I mean I can feel it, but it's not heavy for me,' I said, sticking out my chest a little as I struggled under the weight.

She laughed, and kissed me on the nose, 'Where would I be without my big strong Danny?'

'Probably in Paris already.'

After Ayamin kissed me the pack didn't feel quite so heavy. Or at least I tried a whole lot harder to pretend it didn't.

Greece in spring on a clear sunny day is probably the closest I've been to heaven on earth. The road took us through forests of cypress, oaks, chestnuts, black pines, citrus trees and olive groves, some budding, and others bending under the weight of their fruits.

We stopped for lunch by a small tree on the roadside which had yellow fruit hanging off it.

'How's the pack?' Ayamin asked.

'Damn heavy,' I said, shaking out my arms.

She laughed and pulled one of the small yellow fruit from the tree.

'Here you go,' she placed the little fruit into my mouth, 'This is lunch.'

The fruit was tangy. Almost like an orange – but more mellow.

As we sat on the roadside and watched cars flash past I had this odd feeling, I'd even say I was content.

After lunch, we passed through a small village and traded Ayamin's coins for a large sack of rice to add to the weight of the pack.

With weary feet the two of us followed a winding country road inland until it ran into a four-laned highway that pointed north.

The pack began to slip down my back as we walked along the highway. It would bump on my legs with every step I took, and no matter how many times I tried to pull it higher it would fall back down again. Trucks roared past us and blew gusts of exhaust fumes into my face, and the sun which had warmed us in the morning made my skin sticky and hot.

Yet none of it seemed to bother Ayamin. It was like she had the GPS co-ordinates of London installed in her feet and they were continually pulling her closer.

She was moving much faster than I was, and I had a blister on my right foot that seemed to be getting bigger.

I let out a big sigh and tried to move faster.

Ayamin turned, 'You okay?'

'I feel like I've got heatstroke, and my right foot wants to murder me – so absolutely splendid.'

She stared at me as she walked, 'What is splendid? What does it mean?'

I sighed again and tried to explain that it was kind of like happy, but I was being sarcastic so in this case it meant the opposite. The explaining sort of made my brain hurt.

Ayamin stopped walking.

When I reached her, she brushed aside my hair and felt my forehead, her hand was blissfully cool.

'You're hot,' she said. Not moving her hand away.

'Stop flirting Ayamin.'

She smiled, but it was only a little one, 'Do you think you can keep walking?'

I nodded; I couldn't think of anything smart to say.

'You lie,' she stood on her toes and kissed my forehead, 'We can find somewhere to rest for the night.'

Instantly I felt better, the weight on my back even seemed lighter. I wrapped her up in a hug. Her arms were around me, but when I looked down her eyes and her feet were still pointed north.

I touched her arm as we stepped back from the hug, 'Ayamin, are you sure?'

She glanced north again, and a sad smile took up her face. I could see the desire in her eyes. I wanted to say I could keep going, but I knew my body was about to fall apart. She tore her gaze from the road and her feet turned to me.

'Let's go find somewhere to camp Danny.'

****

Our first Greek campsite was on a little strip of grass beside a stream that wound along a dirt track we'd followed from the highway.

I dropped the pack off my back and fell forwards onto the grass.

'Oh man,' I groaned, 'I am dead.'

'Poor Danny,' Ayamin knelt behind me and massaged my shoulders. Something in my back clicked and I gave a moan as I felt my body relax.

Near the stream was a small stone firepit, Ayamin pointed to it, 'How do you feel about rice, spice, and oranges for dinner?'

'You wouldn't happen to have a steak hiding in that pack would you?'

Ayamin laughed, 'Let me check.'

She stood and pulled the straps, the pack got half a meter off the ground before she dropped it with a thud.

'Danny, how did you manage to carry that?!'

I just let out a moan from where I lay on the ground.

Ayamin ran over and practically jumped on me, 'I'm sorry Danny,' she said, 'I didn't realise it was that heavy.'

She clung to me like a koala bear, 'You should've said something.'

I combed a hand through her hair, 'It's okay. I mean now it's mostly just my neck that hurts.'

She reached out and brushed her fingers on a spot on the side of my neck, 'Here?'

'Yeah. I mean it's not that...'

My sentence broke in two as Ayamin leaned forward and placed her lips on my neck, right where she'd touched me. Her lips were soft and tingled on my skin.

Ayamin sat up with a wicked grin.

'Does that feel better?'

'Uh-ha,' I managed to say. Then turned my neck slightly, 'But the other side is still a bit sore.'

She laughed, and brushed her fingers against my neck again, 'Here?'

'That's the spot.'

Ayamin's kiss lingered this time, I felt her breath on my skin, and her face brushed my chin.

'Better?'

'Yes better...' I bit my lip, 'Only I have sore shoulders as well, you know how the pack pulls them.'

'I'm going to get sore lips with all this kissing I'm doing.'

'That's okay,' I brushed her lips with a finger, 'Here?'

She laughed, and then I kissed her. It was warm and sweet and I could feel her smiling underneath.

****

We woke underneath a damp blanket in a wet tent.

It hadn't rained in the night, Ayamin's pack just had so much water in it that the tent, blankets, and clothes inside hadn't been able to dry before we went to bed.

But the minute that hot summer sun came up we flopped outside onto the grass and began to sunbathe.

'I think we need at least another day of drying,' Ayamin said as steam rose up from our clothes, 'Let's stay here for the night, regather our strength.'

It was rice again for breakfast, then sunbathing until lunch. After crab apples and (more) rice I dipped the tip of my foot into the stream. It was cool, but not cold. Perfect for a swim.

'Perhaps we can just stay here forever,' I pulled my shirt off, 'I could build us a house, we can swim in the stream, and sunbathe in the grass all day.'

'I've got one condition,' Ayamin said from her seat on the grass, 'Our house has to have a yellow door.'

I nodded, and stood leaning over the water in just my boxers. I crouched, prepared to jump, then stopped and turned to her.

'Hey Aya? Why a yellow door?'

'It's like the sun, you know? It brightens up your day, it welcomes you in,' she walked over, scooped up a handful of water, and let it drip through her fingers, 'Our house had a yellow door.'

The water drops made little ripples in the stream as they landed. I could see her reflection in the little ridges as they spread outwards.

She smiled, crouched, and together we jumped.

****

The pack felt like it was made of air when I slipped it back on. We followed the stream back towards the highway, then we followed the highway to the border. It took us a week and a half of walking to get there and as time wore on I began to notice things about my body.

I felt healthy, my legs didn't ache when I walked, and I found I was smiling, even if our diet was rice, rice, and... more rice.

Ayamin and I talked the whole time. We talked about music and movies and high school and history and about each other and made wild schemes for the future.

Finally, the archway that leads into North Macedonia appeared on the horizon. Beyond it were clean green fields and a road of grey tarmac climbing into the distance. *A traveller's heaven.*

But then, as the gate loomed in front of us we looked to our left and saw a very familiar sight.

Hundreds of ramshackle tents littered the field to our left. There seemed to be waves of them, almost crashing like the sea against the border wall. People with raggedy clothes and dirty faces moved through the tents. In a corner some men wearing bandanas were digging a trench, others threw up over it.

Ayamin looked from the tents to me, her eyes narrowed slightly and her head dipped just a little.

'Let's keep going.' I told her, 'We don't know what they'll say at the gate.'

We joined the line at the gate just as a group of Greeks passed through. The next group to approach the guard dragged big white sacks through the mud. They had holes in the knees of their pants and their skin was the same almost olive shade as Ayamin's.

A large guard who'd let the Greeks through barely looked at the crumpled paperwork the Syrian group gave him. He pointed out towards the rows of tents to his left.

The head of the group shook his head and tried to explain, but the large guard just kept pointing in the direction of the camp and repeating a phrase over and over again. It sounded a lot like *go home.*

The man with holes in the knees of his pants tried to shout over the guard, who waved his finger in front of the Syrian man's face. *Go home.*

The Syrian man stared at the guard's finger, he reached up, wrapped a hand around it, and squeezed.

The large guard gave a shout and there was a shuffle as four more blue-uniformed guards appeared beside him. They carried batons in their hands.

The Syrian paused for a moment, the guard's finger was still clutched in his hand. Veins crisshaven't-crossed the Syrian's arm. If he'd given the slightest twist he would've broken the man's finger.

Instead he let go, took his daughter by the hand and led the group towards the makeshift camp beside the road.

When we reached the front of the line, the guard's eyes skipped over Aya then rested on me, before returning to Ayamin again. He paused. Then said something in a language I couldn't understand.

Ayamin shook her head, 'English?'

The man nodded, '*Some...* You have identification?'

Both of us shook our heads, and his eyes narrowed, 'No identification, no come in,' he said, then pointed at Ayamin, 'No Syrian.'

I frowned, 'What do you mean no Syrian?'

The guard just shook his head, 'No Syrian.'

'Where will they go?' Next to me, Ayamin's hand was on my arm, 'There are sick people here, don't you care?'

But the man couldn't understand, or chose not to. His four buddy-guards marched over. They spoke to each other in Macedonian. But stood with the arms crossed, making it pretty clear we weren't going to pass.

Our feet squelched in the mud as we walked to the makeshift camp. Ayamin held my arm, I was still angry, but the further we walked the more it faded into a kind of sadness.

The entire camp – from the tents to the ground was a muddy brown, like all the green had been trampled out by the hundreds that called it home. Little pools of water sat in the holes made by people's footsteps.

We found a quiet corner near the woods and slowly set up our tent.

Eventually we had our faded Winnie the Pooh keeping watch as we climbed inside. Ayamin threw off her boots and lay on the inflatable mattress. She sighed, then held a hand to her eyes. I lay down on the mattress beside her, staring up at the roof.

'What a crap day.'

Her fingers touched my forearm then slid down, across my palm and into my hand.

'Danny?' Her voice was so soft I could barely hear it, 'Can I be negative for a moment?'

'I'm all ears.'

'I don't think we're going to make it.'

I paused for a moment, I could hear the sound of her breathing, and the squelch of someone walking outside.

'Okay... That's too negative, how about something more insulting than negative – like calling those guards a gang of assholes.'

I reached up a hand and brushed the side of her face, 'We'll get past them. Don't you worry.'

She laughed for a beat, but her tears were starting, 'After that someone else is going to try to stop us, and then someone after that. Everyone hates us.'

'Everyone's an asshole then.'

I reached out and held Ayamin. Her quiet sobs shook her chest.

I didn't say anything, I just held her tighter. It felt like I was trying to hold her together.

****

We slept until the sun was well up. Ayamin wouldn't let me leave the tent. She clung to me.

'Just stay here.' she said, hugging herself to my body.

'But... aren't you hungry?' I asked.

She shook her head, 'I feel sort of sick. Besides... you're *always* hungry.'

I touched Aya's forehead. It wasn't particularly hot. But I decided my stomach could wait. I leant my head back on the pillow. Ayamin half smiled, but it looked a little sad. She squeezed up to me and kissed me on the mouth.

'I love you.'

It wasn't long until she was asleep again.

As hard as I tried to shut my eyes, I couldn't join her. Instead I lay awake and stared at the seams of our tent. I decided they needed repairing. They were fine in the sun, but there were small tears where rain would leak through.

My stomach growled and I tried to focus on the tent. We had no food left in our packs – we'd been meaning to buy some when we hit North Macedonia.

A tap on the side of our tent interrupted my thought train.

I checked Ayamin, saw she was still asleep and slipped my arm out from under her. Gently I unzipped the front door of our tent. There stood a wrinkled Syrian woman with a child squirming in her arms.

'Hello,' she said in Arabic.

'Hello.'

She nodded, and then said a sentence too fast for me to get the whole of it.

The two words I did manage to understand were '*food*' and '*want?*' and my stomach was rumbling and that was all I needed to know.

'Yes! Akeed.'

The woman grinned and pointed in the direction of a tent just opposite us. I spun around and shook Ayamin slightly.

'Aya, food.'

When she didn't move, I shook her a little more urgently.

She let out a moan, 'I'm okay. Danny, you go and eat something.'

I peered out of the tent, 'It's not far...'

But Ayamin just pulled the blanket over her head, 'I'm fine. Go!'

I slipped out of our tent and went to join the woman. She gestured to her daughter who was mixing flour and water together. Around us sat a group of excited skinny kids, they all had sticks and were talking and laughing over top of each other.

The woman smiled at me then grabbed one of her grandsons by his collar, spoke in his ear, then pushed him in my direction.

The little boy glanced up at me then lowered his eyes, 'Hello good sirs,' he said in a very English accent, 'Grandma wants to know what you is doing here.'

I nodded to the little boy, 'I'm walking to England.'

The boy turned and told the old lady who seemed to take it as a fair reason. She pointed to where the flour and water were being rolled into a sticky dough and began speaking in Arabic.

The boy looked up at me, 'Grandma says you must eat with us, but first you must find a stick.'

I thanked the little boy and his grandma with a smile and a bow. The group of boys who'd gathered around the tent pulled me towards the woods for a 'stick hunt'.

We ended up climbing a smooth tree so high that we could see the whole camp.

While the view from above was no less brown, I could see slightly over the Macedonian border and the green, green trees and fields over there gave me hope.

I also spotted a small stream near our camp, refugees in boots were drawing water from it into pots for their campfires.

As the boys ran back to their tent, I stopped by Winnie the Pooh and checked up on Aya. As I unzipped the door, I heard her roll over. She lay on her side with her eyes shut.

'Ayamin?' I said, 'Hey Aya.' She didn't move so I poked her with my stick, 'Hey lazy bones.'

She groaned and stretched as she looked at me, 'What is it?'

'Are you doubly, triply sure you don't want any? They're mixing up dough and we're going to roast it over a fire with sticks – it's like camping.'

Aya groaned, 'I'm good – I feel like I'm already getting the full camping experience.'

I laughed, then crawled over and kissed her cheek, 'I won't be long.'

She shook her head, 'Be long. Enjoy yourself.'

I raced out of our tent and back to the fire. Even Ayamin couldn't keep my stomach away from that baked dough. I stood in line with the little boys, each of us groaning and drooling in anticipation.

The woman who'd kneaded the dough wrapped some around the stick I'd found, then the grandma walked up to her and said something in Arabic, the woman loaded it up a little more.

It was starting to get dark by the time we toasted our dough over the fire. I realised that I hadn't eaten all day and had to fight my stomach not to eat the raw dough there and then.

When it was cooked the wait was more than worth it though. The hot substance filled my stomach and brought a smile to each of our faces. The grandma sat back, eating her portion with a content smile.

She turned to the boy who'd spoken to me before and said something.

He stuffed the last piece of his bread in his mouth and spoke through it, 'Grandma says the family is fed, her job today is finished.'

I gazed into the woman's eyes, 'Thank you.'

Grandma smiled, she spoke to the boy again.

'Grandma is worried about the girl who shares tent with you. The mud gets to people – makes them sleepy all the time.'

I frowned, 'How long have you been here?'

The boy counted on his fingers, 'Maybe two months... We get cold sometimes and sick sometimes... but Grandma keeps us going.'

I nodded and looked up at the woman, 'Thanks for your food.'

The bread was still warm in my hands as I walked back to our tent. I could've eaten the whole thing ten times over, but I held myself back, I'd saved half for Ayamin.

I unzipped the door and crawled into our tent. Ayamin lay on her back staring up at the ceiling. She smiled at me, 'Hey Danny.'

I held the bread in my palms. Presenting it to her like it was a golden ring.

'We cooked it on sticks over the fire,' I said.

Aya smiled again and broke off just a small piece, she put it between her lips and gently chewed, she nodded, then wrapped her arms around me, 'Thanks Danny.'

'You want more?' I asked, staring at the lump still in my hand.

She shook her head.

'But... are you sure?' I whispered, my stomach was already beginning to growl.

'I'm sure,' she laughed, 'Go on, eat it Danny.'

'Don't do this to me,' I held it out to her and shut my eyes, 'Please, eat it Ayamin.'

'Danny...' she broke off a piece of bread and put it in my mouth, 'I can't eat any more. It's yours.'

That was all the encouragement I needed, that bread was gone in half a minute and I lay back, already feeling guilty.

'Are you sure you don't want anything?' I asked, 'You haven't really eaten.'

Ayamin shook her head, then stopped, 'Actually there is something I need,' she said, a grin touching on her face.

'What's that?'

She nibbled at my ear, 'I need you to love me Danny.'

'But I do!'

She laughed, then kissed my mouth, she tasted sweet, 'But not enough.'

Ayamin slowly pushed up my t-shirt and began to kiss my chest. I groaned and grinned all in one, Ayamin lay flat on my chest.

'Do you think we could stay like this forever?' she said

I kissed her again, 'Mmmh... I don't know I think I'd get hungry.'

She giggled, 'We've got everything we need right here.'

I laughed.

I thought she was joking.

****

The next morning, I woke with Ayamin's arms wrapped around me, and my stomach groaning like sailors about to mutiny.

I yawned and peered out the door of the tent, there was a thick wall of rain clouds approaching us.

'Aya,' I said, touching her face.

Her warm body shifted and her arms clung to me a little tighter, 'I'm sleeping.'

'Come on Aya, if you stay in bed much longer, you'll never leave.'

She groaned, 'That's the plan.'

I laughed, then I remembered the stream running alongside the camp I'd seen yesterday.

With Ayamin protesting I slipped myself out of her arms, and half stood – which is about all you could do in the Winnie the Pooh tent.

I reached down and lifted Ayamin like a bride.

'What are you doing?' she said as I lifted her through the door and walked with her down the rows of tents.

I just gave a little smile, then as we neared the stream, she began to scream, 'No, no Danny, no please...'

I held her over it and she clung to my chest, 'Please... I'll come out of the tent, I'll make you fresh omelettes every morning, I'll love you until the day I die...'

I cocked my head to the side, 'Hmmm... very appealing... but...'

I opened my arms and Ayamin fell into the stream, it wasn't particularly cold, but it was rather wet, I stood on the side laughing, and waited for her to drag me in.

But when she surfaced Ayamin was quiet, she didn't yell, just heaved herself onto the bank and began to cry.

****

It isn't easy to completely blank someone for two days straight, and I would've thought it was damn near impossible when you both share an air mattress in a tent smaller than most bedrooms.

Yet somehow Ayamin managed it. No matter how many times I apologised she wouldn't look, or even speak to me. Those nights were the first that she hadn't cuddled up to me and I felt the loss of her warmth.

Two days after I'd thrown her into the stream, I decided to go to the nearest town and buy supplies. I counted off the last few coins she'd given me.

'I'm going to find us something to eat, Ayamin... I'll miss you.'

She lay on the mattress re-reading *Two Hearts in the French Night*. Her face was practically buried beneath the yellow daisy on the cover and she didn't even lift her head.

I walked to the town, and it felt weird walking alone. I decided I was going to buy Ayamin the biggest loaf of bread I could find.

After a ten-kilometre hike, I found that even the town's cheapest baking nearly doubled my scrawny stash of money. In the end, all I could afford was a sack of rice and six beans.

As I lugged the sack of rice back to our little tent I couldn't stop thinking about Ayamin being mad. I gazed down at the road and felt my ribs. I was hungry, my girl semi-hated me, and we were probably going to remain in that muddy bog in front of the wall for the rest of our days.

I groaned and kicked at the ground. It was probably going to start raining soon. My arms were sore from carrying the rice.

I sat on a rock with my sack of rice and gazed around. There was the road, worn down by traffic. On it, a small truck rattled on by.

To my left, I saw a burst of purple and orange. Climbing down from the rock I discovered it was a patch of wildflowers, hidden from the road.

Gently, I pulled a few flowers from the plants. They were pretty and at the same time survivors, just like Ayamin. I gathered more and more and started laughing as I imagined Ayamin's reaction. I also found a wild yellow sunflower to give to the grandma who'd fed me.

When I had more than I could carry I picked up the sack of rice and began walking once more. It didn't feel so heavy.

As cars passed, I burst into random fits of laughter as I imagined her reaction to the flowers. I made it back to the camp and found that for once Ayamin wasn't in our tent.

Grinning to myself I put the rice in our bag and arranged the flowers on the air mattress, orange purple, orange, purple in the most colourful heart Ayamin would've ever seen. Then I sat outside the tent threading two flower crowns as I waited for Aya to come back.

A while later her head popped into our row of tents and I hid the just-finished crowns behind my back. She walked towards me taking dainty bites on a piece of campfire bread. My stomach rumbled.

I kept a smile on my face as she moved closer. There was a little more colour on her face than there had been in a while. When her eyes met mine, a smile started to creep onto her lips, but she caught it at the last moment.

She stepped past me, unzipped Winne the Pooh, and climbed inside. Then she stopped, half-in and half-out of the tent.

There was silence. My hands began to feel clammy where I was holding the flower crowns.

A moment later Ayamin bounced out of the tent and tackled me into the ground, wrapping her arms around me.

She was yelling something in Arabic, which I'm pretty sure meant *I love you.* She laughed and kissed my face.

I brushed aside a few stray hairs from her face and placed the flower crown so it sat on her ears. Ayamin giggled and kissed me again.

She took the second flower crown from my hands and carefully squeezed it onto my head. Then we lay on the dirt and laughed.

****

That night it began to rain.

Ayamin cooked us the best rice and beans I had ever tasted. When we finished eating, I took my shirt off and sat, totally blissed-out at the feeling of a full belly.

As the first fat drops of water hit the dirt around our tent Ayamin put the bowls outside for the rain to wash, then pulled me close to her. She kissed my chin, then rolled so her head rested on my chest.

I ran my hand through her long, dark, almost wild hair and Ayamin sighed.

'I'm sorry for being mad Danny.'

Her hand reached out and took mine. I shook my head, 'I shouldn't have chucked you in the stream.'

'I just wanted to drown in my despair for a little while, but you wouldn't let me. Would you?'

She squeezed my hand and I breathed in and the words rolled right off my heart.

'I love you.'

She stared down my chest at me, then her head moved and she was kissing me, hot and passionate right on the mouth. We kept kissing until we'd probably set a new world record for breath-holding.

As we broke away, she brushed her nose with mine, 'I love you.'

I reached out and handed her one of the flowers that lay beside our bed, it was purple and rounded, but if you half closed your eyes it almost looked like a rose.

Ayamin took it and kissed me again. Her hands ran down my chest. The rain beat a tango on the roof of our tent. That night was one to remember.

****

I'm not really the sort of guy who reads a bible or even gives a hoot about what's in it. But when you're a foster child you've got to do whatever your foster family is doing, and there were a whole load of churchy foster families. Enough that I learnt the story of Noah and his ark.

That's what I dreamt about as the sound of rain woke me the next morning – I dreamt that Ayamin and I were the last humans on earth. We were sailing the world in a Winnie the Pooh shaped raft and would eventually have to repopulate the planet – a task I decided I would be rather looking forward to.

After that dream ended, I opened my eyes to what at first seemed like bliss. The back of Ayamin's body rested against mine, the heat of her back made me warm, even without either of us wearing a t-shirt and I could feel her every heartbeat through her soft skin.

I didn't really want to get up but my throat was dry. As I hopped off the inflatable mattress my feet sunk up to the ankles in cold muddy water.

Blinking, I half wondered if I was still dreaming about Noah's ark.

But then I unzipped the front door and another layer of water slipped into our tent. I got a glimpse of thick brown water swirling through the camp. Raindrops pelted people as they left their tents.

'Ayamin?' I called, sloshing water as I spun around.

'Mmh,' she said.

'I think we're going to have to move the tent.'

Ayamin stretched out. Her hand dipped into the water on the side of our bed, she opened her eyes, 'Oh damn.'

'It's still raining as well.'

We stuffed everything dry into the pack and attempting to drain the water from our tent by lifting one side. After pulling out our poles and pegs, we threw everything onto the inflatable mattress and pushed it like a raft toward the border road. It was then, that we noticed the barrier.

A large orange fence had been erected on either side of the road. A mob of refugees had gathered on the camp side of the fence, some of them were shouting.

Ayamin tapped the arm of a woman whose hijab was soaked and sticking to her face, 'What's happening?'

The woman pointed to the road and let out a stream of words too fast for me to understand. She looked like she wanted to cry. She kept talking until a little boy, probably no older than four tugged at her side. She picked him up out of the water.

Ayamin turned to me, 'They've blocked us from the road, they don't want refugees holding up the traffic.'

I shook my head, 'It's the only ground above the water. What about us?"

Ayamin stared at the fence, 'I don't think we matter.'

Near the orange fence, the young refugee men were getting frantic. They shouted strings of curse words at the guards, who had brought in something that vaguely reminded me of a bazooka.

I took Ayamin's hand as the men picked up rocks and mud from beneath the water and begin pelting the guards.

The grenade launcher went bang and what looked like a bomb exploded near the young men, showering them in a cloud of smoke. Refugees began to run, coughing as they went. Some reached down to the water at their feet and began splashing it frantically on their faces.

The grenade launcher turned to us and Ayamin grabbed my arm, 'Tear gas,' she yelled, 'Let's get the hell out of h-'

Ayamin was cut short as a shell exploded above us. She pulled her semi-wet t-shirt over her face, while I, in my stupidity, stared at the white vapour that leaked from it.

As the first drops hit my eyes I blinked, the sensation was like getting soap in them, and my nose and my mouth felt like I'd been snorting pepper. As Ayamin pulled me away the burning slowly increased until my eyes were watering so much I couldn't see.

Ayamin dragged me until the screams of the people behind us had quietened. She told me to sit down and I felt the inflatable mattress underneath me. My skin stung and snot bubbled from my nose.

'Ahhhh,' I screamed, rubbing my eyes.

'No!' Ayamin shouted, slapping my hand away, 'That'll only make it worse. I'll get you to the stream, but you need to blink those tears away.'

I did as she said, and my eyes began to clear slightly, but still stung like hell. With my eyes now open, I saw Ayamin was also blinking away.

'Did they get you too?'

She shrugged, 'Yeah, but it's not as scary if it's happened to you before.' She wiped at her nose, 'My first time, I thought I'd gone blind.'

She took my hand, and helped me up from our inflatable mattress/life raft, then pulled me towards the stream. There were already a couple of people there, lying face down in the water with just their underwear on.

'Time to strip,' Ayamin said, throwing off her clothes.

As I took my clothes off the stinging around my body increased. It was like having saltwater poured into a thousand little cuts. The moment I was down to boxers I let myself fall face-first into the swollen stream.

The current carried me a few meters before I clung to the side of the bank. I opened my eyes then instantly squeezed them closed as what felt like little needles plunged into my eyeballs. But quickly the water carried the stinging away. By the time Ayamin and I came up for air, we were smiling again.

Ayamin allowed the current to drag her down to me, and little raindrops clung to her skin as she settled beside me.

'Congrats,' she said, 'You're no longer a tear gas virgin. How was it?'

I shook my head, 'I don't even think swearing my head off would begin to describe it.'

She laughed and wiped her nose before she hugged me, 'I guess though you're getting the true refugee experience, right?'

I wrapped my arms around her, 'Yeah, lucky I was here to protect you just then.'

Ayamin laughed, then brought her lips to my forehead, 'You're my hero Danny.'

****

Even together, the stream quickly became too cold for us. We picked up our clothes and waded back to our inflatable mattress in the rain. Here we were faced with our original problem.

The stream had burst its banks, water reached the tops of our feet, and we couldn't go anywhere. But we couldn't live in a flooded tent.

Ayamin shivered as I found her rain jacket in the pack. She leant against me and we held the jacket like a roof above us as we planned our next move. Around us, people were coughing in their flooded tents.

I heard the sounds of mothers trying to hush wailing children, and young women yelling at their teargassed husbands. After the craziness of the last few hours, I began to feel a cold disappointment begin to sink in. Ayamin shivered, and I pulled her closer to me. For once our combined warmth wasn't enough to take the edge off the cold. She still shivered and so did I.

While we stood, we saw an old man emerge from the stand of trees on the other side of the stream. He carried a long thick stick to his tent and pulled out a small pocketknife. In ten minutes, he had sharpened the end of his stick to a blade. Then, using the stick like a shovel, he began mounding up the mud into a square patch around his tent.

Ayamin and I watched. Within a few minutes he'd dug enough mud to make a small barrier around his tent and other people were emerging from the woods with sticks of their own.

Without a word, Ayamin and I were on our feet and moving towards the woods. We crossed the swollen stream using a fallen tree and crossed back over with two soon to be digging sticks. Ayamin found a place where the water level only came up to the bottom of her ankle and I sharpened the two sticks.

We began to dig. Both of us mounding up mud into a little platform.

By the time midday had arrived, we had created a soft squishy base for our tent that hung a few centimetres out of the water.

'Lunch?' Ayamin said, handing me the pot of boiled rice from the night before.

I was sort of in two minds about the boiled rice. One, I was starting to hate it because rice seemed to be all we ever ate, and two, in that moment I loved it because being teargassed, mounding mud, and freezing your ass off are great ways to work up an appetite.

As we munched, I watched the family who'd given me the campfire bread when we'd arrived. The family had just finished unpacking two of their tents and were beginning to unpack a third. The grandma's two sons came out of the tent carrying an older man in a wheelchair.

They carried him past their growing mound to a small pile of rocks they'd set up. The family stretched a small tarpaulin over the man in the wheelchair, and the grandma gave him a little food as work on the family's mound continued.

It looked like they'd started later than us and probably wouldn't finish before nightfall.

I looked at Ayamin, her hair and her shirt and everything were muddy and drenched, I was no better. The two of us were placing rocks on the sides of our mound to keep the mud from washing away when we sat our tent on it.

Ayamin dumped the last few rocks in place, then washed her hands in the brown water that surrounded us.

'Phew,' she said, 'I am dead.'

I shook my worn-out arms, 'Then you're not going to be so keen on my next suggestion.'

Ayamin groaned, 'You want us to make the mound two stories high with an air condition garage below?'

I laughed, 'Love the idea... but no,' I pointed to the family, 'I'm not sure if they'll make it before dark.'

Ayamin rubbed her back, she'd worked hard, harder than I'd seen anybody work. She'd been tear-gassed, and only thought of me. The rain was still licking the ground around us and most people would've been crying to go indoors in that moment.

But Ayamin, she just nodded, 'If they want our help, we give it to them.'

She trudged through the muddy water and grabbed her stick. I shook my head, it's a little cliché but I knew then, I truly knew, that I was in love with her.

She took my hand and together we walked to the grandma's tent.

****

We dug for hours.

Initially, the family's two teenage boys tried to race each other. Scooping as fast as they could, but even the boys slowed when they realised the task ahead of us.

It became a rhythmic shovelling of dirt on our long spearlike sticks. I remembered back to England where we had proper shovels and spades.

Truth be told, if I had a shovel at that point, I'd probably trade it for anything (except rice) to eat.

Occasionally as we shovelled, we talked, Ayamin told me the family were from the south of Syria and had left the country two years ago. At the family's centre was the woman I'd been calling Grandma and her wheelchair-bound husband who sat shivering underneath a tarpaulin while the rain came down.

The old couple had two sons: Mahdi and Jamal, who were joined by their wives Rima and Yara and eight grandchildren between them.

They'd been hungry, been beaten, been robbed, yet they considered themselves lucky. They'd all made it alive.

'Even him,' she pointed at the grandfather in the wheelchair peeking out from beneath the tarpaulin.

The man in the wheelchair fascinated me. Our journey had been brutally tough and terrifying and I imagined how much harder his must have been to come all this way without being able to take a step.

The sun was still up as we neared completion, and the older man spoke to one of the kids.

The kid turned to me, 'He says you are a good work,' then Aya as well, 'You both are.'

I nodded, 'I'm impressed by him.'

The kid translated it and the man shook his head, he said something and this time Ayamin translated.

'He doesn't think he was brave to come here. He says he just had to. He says he wouldn't have survived if he'd been left alone, so he might as well be with the family he loves.'

The man stared at me, right in the eyes, his were almost grey. They looked like they'd seen the world.

I nodded, and he did too. We didn't need anyone to translate that for us.

To finish the tent bases we scrambled around in the water for rocks and piled them around the edges. Then we washed our hands in the water and said goodbye.

Grandma, bless her soul, was trying to hand us things for doing the work. First, it was a nice walking pole they'd found, then a root which they thought might be a potato, and even a few of her family's dwindling stash of coins.

We shook our heads, I put an arm around Ayamin's shoulder and we walked back to Winnie the Pooh. The inside of our tent was damp, our mattress was damp, and just about everything in it had been affected by the water.

Only the pack had semi-escaped the water's wrath. We pulled on a few pieces of dry clothing and I used my remaining shirt to dry the top of our bed. Water dripped from the roof onto us as we lay there. Both of us were sniffing, and my throat was feeling even drier than when I woke up. I rolled closer to Aya to keep warm, and also because I loved her.

There was no way in the world we were going to get a fire going so we opened the sack of rice and just swallowed each grain raw which normally is a bad idea, but we needed something to fill the gap. The little grains grated on my throat.

As we lay there Ayamin turned and laid her hand on my arm.

'I'm glad you're here Danny.'

I touched her face, 'I'm glad you're here Aya.'

She nestled into my chest and despite the rain still beating away at Winnie the Pooh above us and the tent being completely soaked, I felt okay. My muscles were exhausted, but with Ayamin's skin next to mine, I didn't feel the aches.

'Goodnight Danny.'

I felt strangely content, it was the same feeling I'd had when we were sitting in the coastguard rooms - like I'd been through the worst and survived. I was just glad the day was over.

'Night Ayamin.'

****

I don't know whether it was the tear gas, submerging ourselves in a cold stream, or spending the night in a saturated tent, but that morning both of us woke up with a cold.

Ayamin groaned, and as she opened her eyes a drop of water had landed on her head.

'Dannyyyyyy,' she rasped, 'My throat is *killing* me.'

I nodded, 'You need some lemons, ginger, and honey - that's like the ultimate cold cure.'

Ayamin laughed, it turned to a cough halfway through, 'Hot chocolate, a sauna, and a warm hotel room wouldn't go amiss.'

As she cuddled into me, I felt her forehead, it was hot. Ayamin's eyes sprang open, 'Don't you dare throw me into that stream again.'

I laugh-coughed, then kissed her forehead, 'Don't worry about that. It might be a good idea to stay in bed today though.'

She nodded and leaned back, 'What are you going to do?'

I shrugged, 'I don't know... something.'

I took off my dry clothes and wrung out the wet ones, then shuddered as I squeezed back into the cold t-shirt. It was depressing putting on wet clothes, but better than going to sleep in them.

I threw on our jacket and unzipped Winnie the Pooh. On the bed, Ayamin groaned as a slight breeze blew into the tent.

I climbed out, zipped up the door, and splashed through the water around our tent. It didn't look like the water had got any higher, but at the same time, it hadn't gone down very much.

Swollen grey rainclouds loomed in every direction.

As I walked, I thought about Ayamin, I'd done a pretty bad job of providing for us - I was basically living off the little money she had.

I decided to head for the town I'd bought our rice in. We needed something nutritious to get us through the colds.

I made it to the village just as the Sunday market opened. I sauntered up to one of the sellers hoping I could convince him to give me some of his leftovers.

The man just held up his hand the moment he saw me and said something in Greek. The only two words I understood were 'no' and 'refugee'.

The other sellers had similar responses.

By the time I'd tried half the market, I was hungry, miserable, and cold. Because I couldn't do anything about the first two, I decided to walk around the town to warm myself up. I felt my chest and felt the bones. I imagined Ayamin and I wasting away. I imagined us on one of those television charity advertisements where you can donate just a dollar a day to help a Danny in need.

As I was feeling sorry for myself, I noticed a lemon tree with plenty of fruit on it. The lemons belonged to a large house with a small brick wall in front of it. The sort of brick wall that I'd be able to leap over in a few steps.

I realised I'd stopped walking. I couldn't see any movement through the windows of the house, just drab old furniture. The branches of the tree were straining with the weight of the lemons. Some were even rotting on the ground.

An image of Aya drinking lemons with honey appeared in my mind. I remembered her cough.

I casually glanced both ways down the street, no one was coming.

I bolted for the lemon tree, leaping the fence with ease. My adrenaline was pumping and a wicked smile filled my face; I'd forgotten how fun stealing was.

I'd been meaning to only take one or two lemons, but I ended up with more than ten. I stuffed them into the pockets of my shirts and even bit down on one so I'd be able to carry it. I leapt back over the fence and casually walked down the road like nothing had happened.

Just as I reached the corner of the street, I heard someone yelling. It sounded like an old man. I pretended not to hear and turned down the next street before breaking into a run.

Standing beside a grey concrete wall. I took my t-shirt off and tied it into a small sack. I placed the lemons in it, then with a grin I walked back down the street.

It was only as I approached the market that I had a brainwave. With a grin, I found a little space beside an overhang and placed the shirt down with eight of my lemons on top.

I glanced around, only one other stall was selling lemons that I could see and they were charging three euros for four which was the same as half a loaf of bread.

I grinned, 'Lemon!'

'Lemon!'

'Lemon!'

Around me, people began to stare, I just fixed them with a smile and gestured to my yellow fruit, 'Lemon!' I called again.

A middle-aged Greek woman with a staunch face came closer, she turned my lemons in her hands and raised an eyebrow.

She said something in Greek that went way over my head, not that it mattered, I just grinned a little wider and said, 'Two lemon one euro.'

The women snorted, picked up four of my lemons and handed me two euro.

'Lemóni,' she said, pointing at the lemons, 'lemóni.'

I picked one up, 'Lemóni?'

She nodded, then placed her lemons in a bag and left.

Armed with my new and improved Greek vocabulary the rest of my lemóni disappeared fast, by midday I was carrying a loaf of bread, two lemons and a little sugar back to Ayamin. I'd been aiming to get her some honey, but even my lemóni weren't enough for that beautiful nectar.

****

After trudging through the water and mud, I climbed into the tent, a massive grin on my face. Ayamin was sleeping, so after putting on my dry clothes I sat the loaf in front of her and gently shook her awake.

Ayamin breathed in and the way she looked at the loaf made my heart sing.

'Danny, what? How??' she said, holding the loaf up like it was worth a million dollars.

I grinned, 'There was a lemóni tree in town, just stacked full of them, I went, took a few and managed to sell them at a market – that's where I got the bread and sugar.'

Ayamin put the loaf down, 'You stole someone's lemons?' she whispered.

'Lemóni,' I corrected, 'And not really, there were so many on the tree – even some on the ground. You needed them way more than any of those people did.'

Ayamin shook her head, 'If they caught you it wouldn't be good for the camp,' her voice grew softer as she gave the loaf another sniff, 'But I still love you for doing it.'

She reached for a plate, and gently cut a quarter each for us, Ayamin was so careful that I swear not even a crumb was wasted.

We sat eating, mouths watering at how good that bread tasted, and how amazing it felt in our stomachs, our coughs seemed to ease just a little after our bellies were full.

'It's strange, Ayamin said, rubbing her stomach, 'I know I couldn't eat one bite more – but my brain's telling me to EAT, EAT, EAT.'

I laughed, 'I could eat a loaf the size of Westminster and I wouldn't even be full.

Ayamin lay back on the bed with a sniff, 'Would you show me the cathedral if we make it to England?'

'What do you mean if?' I grinned, 'Girl, we're going there no matter what.' Ayamin laughed and I pointed outside the tent, 'I don't care what those border guards think, stuff them, stuff all of them. I promise on... on my *life* that I'm going to get you to England.'

I expected Ayamin to laugh, or smile or something. Instead, she burst into tears. Big fat sobbing tears.

I reached for her, a little scared, the tears kept rolling as she touched my face, 'Oh Danny, you stupid sweet idiot,' she said.

'Hey!' I said, feeling a tear or two of my own begin to well up – even though I didn't know why, 'What'd I say?'

Ayamin hugged me to her, 'You don't even know!' she said, 'Oh Danny.'

While she cried some more and I wrapped my arms around her the rainclouds raged on and our tent leaked above us and I decided that it was time. We couldn't stay here forever. Ayamin's cold would only get worse.

From tomorrow, I thought as I watched her hair rise and fall on my chest. *From tomorrow I'm going to find out how to make it past the border.*

****

When we woke the rain had stopped. Around us, the stream and campsite were still flooded, but the water only reached the tips of my boots when I went to collect sticks for a fire. Despite all the wood being soaked I managed to make Ayamin a lemon and sugar, and by just after midday the sun had begun to shine once more, drying out our tents.

While Ayamin and I hung a few of our clothes and blankets on the tent to dry we watched a gathering of refugee men disappear into the forest.

'I wonder where they're going?' I said.

Ayamin turned to a kid who was carrying a load of sticks past our tent and asked him. When he was finished telling her she turned to me.

'They're searching for a way around.'

I nodded, a smile forming on my face.

'Have they found anything?' I asked the kid.

He seemed a little surprised at me speaking but told me they had just begun a few hours ago and he didn't know.

As the boy disappeared, I turned to see Ayamin staring at me, a funny expression on her face.

'What?' I asked, folding a t-shirt on Winnie the Pooh's nose.

'Your Arabic is getting pretty good,' she said.

'What do you mean?'

'Well, you managed to ask that kid if they'd found something without completely butchering the words.'

'Wait what?' I thought back, it hadn't felt like I was speaking Arabic, 'Are you sure?'

'Positive,' she laughed, 'How do you think he understood you?'

While Ayamin disappeared back inside the tent, I stood frozen, still holding my shirt. *I'm semi-good at a language,* I thought. My eyebrows wrinkled a little and then slowly a smile slipped onto my face. Right through school I'd never excelled at much, my exam scores ranged from *bad* and *very bad* to *did not attend because buying cigarettes was more important.* Yet somehow, I'd managed to learn a language in just a few months.

The smile grew wider and... I felt proud.

We'd eaten the rest of the bread, and finished off the other half of a lemon when the men arrived back at camp. They moved as a group before dispersing into their tents.

I tried to ask what they'd found as they passed, but they just shook their heads. Standing next to me, Ayamin looked worried.

It was only the next night that we found out what was happening. We heard a tapping on the side of our tent, Ayamin unzipped the door, and in popped the head of the grandma whose site we'd helped build. In her hand, she held a small roll of campfire bread.

She handed it to Ayamin then beckoned her closer. The grandma whispered into Ayamin's ear for a minute or two then looked at me, gave a wink, then disappeared from our tent.

Aya zipped up the door then leaned closed to me on the mattress, 'So apparently they think you're a North Macedonian spy.'

I frowned, 'A spy? Why would I do that?'

She shrugged, 'I don't know.... You're the spy, you tell me,' I stared at Aya until she started laughing, 'These people are just worried.'

'So they won't tell us how to get through?'

She shook her head, 'Fortunately, you made friends with the right family, the grandma told me they're leaving when dark falls tomorrow night.'

I grinned, 'And we'll just sneak along?'

'Yep, we'll just sneak along.'

****

You could feel the tension in the air the next morning. An outsider would think nothing of it, but the fact there was no laughter, no screaming said a lot. The camp was mute.

Ayamin and I packed up everything inside our half-dry tent and left the outside completely untouched. Occasionally I'd glance at the border guards. They didn't seem to notice us.

None of the refugees spoke to me, but at the same time, no one told us not to come. In my mind that was about as good an invite as we were going to get.

As night approached, Ayamin and I were rearing to go. We sat in our tent talking about leaving the mud behind.

Darkness fell and we began to hear soft Arabic voices and the clinking of metal as tents were packed away.

Ayamin and I crawled from ours, dragging the backpack behind us. We had our poles folded up and pegs stashed away by the time the first families began to leave. Someone had judged the night perfectly, and there were only clouds in the sky, with no moon to light us up.

Ayamin and I stuffed the fabric of the tent into the pack, and I hoisted it onto my back – groaning just a little, 'I don't remember it being this heavy,' I said.

Ayamin poked me in the shoulder, 'You've just got lazy, that's why.'

I reached for her, but she darted away, 'See slowpoke?'

Then with white teeth grinning in the night, we made our way towards the forest.

The fallen tree over the stream sat in place, but it was hard to balance in the near-darkness. A woman in the family in front of us had a dim torch that they shone to help us cross.

'Thank you,' I said in Arabic. The man beside her smiled until the dull light showed my face, then he turned to the woman.

'Turn around, let's go,' he said to her, before letting out an angry string of words that I didn't ask Ayamin to translate for me.

'I'm guessing he's not my biggest fan.' I whispered as I helped Ayamin over a branch that blocked the path.

We followed the pinpricks of light and the trail that another group had left, stumbling and falling over sticks and stumps and shrubs until we reached what was basically the entire population of the camp all gathered upon the riverbank.

Wary eyes turned to us and some people murmured a little to each other. I gazed at the river, pretending I didn't see it

While latecomers continued to arrive, the camp watched two men tie a long rope around the waist of a fit-looking, sixteen-year-old guy.

When the rope was secured, an older man called out and everyone with a torch aimed it at the river. The rope guy took a series of breaths, then plunged into the fast-moving water.

His head broke through the surface and he began swimming long freestyle strokes towards the other shore. It wasn't until he reached the middle that he began to drift downriver.

The men on our side continued letting out the rope until the teenager had washed up on the other bank. He was ten meters further downstream than where he'd started. As he hauled himself up, everyone around us gave a small cheer for him. Ayamin took my hand as the men on our side tied the rope onto a sturdy looking tree, 'It's going to be freezing.' she whispered.

I nodded, 'How about we just sneak into first class on a train?'

She grinned, 'Champagne and decent food would be a hardship, but I guess it's one we could bear.'

I stared up at the sky, she looked across the water, 'One step closer to England,' she whispered.

The guy who'd swum across ran up the riverbank until he was standing opposite us. He wrapped the rope around the base of a sturdy tree once, twice, three times then tied it off and gave the thumbs up.

Whole families with the kids riding on their parents' shoulders began to slosh through the water. When the current caught them our fellow refugees clung to the rope that had been set up, using it to drag themselves across.

I spotted my campfire bread family down by the water and nudged Ayamin, 'Come on, let's go.'

We stood to our feet and moved to the water's edge. The grandma was trying to organise everybody. One of her sons had to take his daughter across, but that only left one son for her husband in the wheelchair.

'We'll have to come back for you,' she was saying. But then she heard our footsteps and the old woman stared at me as I came to a stop in front of her.

I smiled and nodded to her and that seemed to be enough.

'England man take him,' Grandma said, pushing her son to the other side of the wheelchair.

I looked from the grandfather to the son and nodded at each of them before the son and I hoisted his father, chair and all, onto our shoulders.

We sloshed into the water. And as it began to fill my boots, I let out a little yell of excitement. The cold had got my adrenaline flowing. I felt strangely alive.

By the time the son and I were reaching the middle we were finding it harder and harder to reach the bottom, the cold water came up to our chests and we began to drift downstream until we hit the rope. It dug into my side as I fought to get a foothold. The son slipped and disappeared under completely. The old man's feet and knees dipped into the water.

I pushed a little further towards the other side before I too felt my head drop beneath the surface. Dark water swirled around me and my arms and shoulders were aching from carrying the grandad, I felt my knee hit rock and that made me kick out instinctively, my foot pushed against the sand and I shot back to the surface. The rope grazed my side as I leant into it. I found my next foothold, took a deep breath and pushed once more. This time I didn't go under.

The son grinned at me and clung to the wheelchair. He was shivering like crazy, but the ground was beginning to slope upward. 'Let's go, let's go!' he whispered.

Behind us, Ayamin held the pack above her head as she emerged from beneath the water.

At the other side two men helped lift the grandfather from our shoulders, we climbed up onto the bank and I slapped hands with the son. Both of us grinned in the cold.

'Well done,' he said in Arabic, and I nodded, 'To you too.'

The grandfather laughed, 'I feel like a king.'

The two of us helped Ayamin get the pack up the bank. When she hugged me I could feel her relief. It wasn't just making it across the river, we'd also left the dreaded field of mud behind.

We shoved on some dry clothes and our wet boots, then she took my hand again, 'Time for the open road!'

One of the men took the lead, and we began walking along a small footpath that led away from the river. I helped the family out with their wheelchair a few times as dawn began to approach, and the grandma helped our stomachs with a snack of seeds.

By the time the sun was up, we'd met a road end. Family groups began to leave with spaces of five minutes between each one and soon Ayamin and I were walking alongside our new adopted family, with Grandma leading us from the front.

****

Our first days in North Macedonia were spent walking through its central valley. The ground was relatively lush and mountain ranges watched over us from a distance.

Progress was much slower travelling with the grandfather. His wheelchair was constantly getting stuck on roots and stones.

The hills were the worst though. Although he wasn't much more than bones and clothing, Grandpa's weight seemed to double every time a slope appeared.

One hill in particular took us nearly two hours to get over, and that was with me and the old man's two sons taking turns to push.

At one point I was nearing the top. My breathing was ragged and I could feel my legs starting to ache.

'I think last night's apple potatoes have gone to your hips Grandpa,' I wheezed.

'Well, they must've gone to yours too boy. Look how slow you're moving.'

I gave an out of breath chuckle and then heard a chugging from behind me. I turned back and watched as a train steamed by. The breeze it stirred up was wonderfully cooling and it gave me a good excuse to pause and catch my breath.

'Damn I wish we were on that train,' I said.

'Damn I wish I had legs,' Grandpa croaked, 'But that ain't happening any time soon.'

I stared at the train... at the wagons of logs moving past us... and then it was gone.

When we crested the hill, I spotted a small train station in the valley below us. The train we'd seen had stopped there, and that gave me an idea.

****

It was night when the train arrived. The slow clack of its wheels bouncing along the track was like a countdown timer. I peered both ways from our little hideout in the grass.

'No one's watching.'

The face of Mahdi, the eldest son, appeared beside me. A wild grin showed on his white teeth. 'Let's go then.'

He ran over to the open sided carriage that was just stopping in front of us. Hundreds of logs were stacked on it, but the steel beams that held them in place gave a narrow shelf to sit on.

Ayamin grabbed my hand and the two of us ran to join him while the grandfather was wheeled over by Mahdi's younger brother.

On the other side of the rails was the dull sound of wood being dropped onto the train. They were filling up the bays fast.

The grandfather was pushed onto the carriage by his two sons, then they helped Grandma climb on. Just as the train gave a blow of its horn Ayamin and the rest of the family piled on. The kids scrambled up the railing like monkeys. I gazed both directions down the railway line, making sure we hadn't been spotted before stepping onto the metal railing and climbing aboard.

'Get back, get hidden,' Mahdi whisper-shouted to us, 'Someone's checking the chains.'

We pressed our backs against the logs, and two of the children held their hands over their eyes. The rattling of chains was distant at first but got closer and closer. *Chi-ching, chi-ching, chi-ching...*

At the back of the train, someone began shouting in Macedonian.

The man who'd been rattling the chains shouted back and then broke into a jog. I held my breath as he passed us by, his eyes focussed on the end of the train.

We heard the two men talking and then some sort of decision must've been reached because the crunch of their footsteps moved back towards the station.

With a jerk, the train began to move off and next to me the family fell to their knees in prayer. Well, most of the family. The youngest was staring at me, he had these big brown eyes. Ayamin and I looked at each other, then back at those eyes full of worry and excitement.

'I've never been on a train before,' he said, 'Do we get to see the conductor?'

The train's horn blew. I took Ayamin's hand and we leant back against the trunks of the beech trees. Their scent washed over us as our railway car left the yard and the cool night air began to make me shiver.

Ayamin reached for our bag, which sat between my knees, flipped the clips and pulled out our blanket, she wrapped it around the two of us. The train clattered on and on.

****

In hindsight it was amazing we lasted as long as we did. But at the time, being discovered by the train guards was like a cold slap of water in the face.

We'd left North Macedonia's wall behind and passed through into Serbia... The sun came out, we passed through stations and countrysides and snacked on a bag of nuts Grandma had been saving.

Just after pulling out of our fifth loading yard, the crop fields whizzing past us began to slow. Within two minutes the train ground to a halt.

'Repairs?' I whispered.

'Animal on the tracks,' Ayamin suggested.

We heard the crunch of multiple boots on the gravel. They were moving quickly.

'Don't move,' Grandma whispered, she clutched one of the children's hands, 'Be brave for me.'

The boots came to a stop, the guards stood there staring at us. There were three of them, they held batons in their hands and hate in their eyes.

One of them was sweating, had a tiny moustache, and seemed to be in charge. He shouted something in a language I couldn't recognise and they advanced, batons drawn.

The first blow from one of the lackeys came swooshing down towards my head. I moved sideways and it caught my collarbone with a dull thud that left a patch of pain.

Two of the women screamed and we tried to back ourselves up but could go no further than the beech logs. I wrapped my arms around Ayamin and rolled so only my back was facing the guards. Their batons hit my ribs and smashed down on my spine.

I felt something crack and breathing became painful.

The kids, sheltered by their fathers, were bawling.

When the beating stopped, a hand grabbed my hair and used it to yank me from the train. The rocks tore into my hands as I hit the side of the railway.

Grandpa, sitting in his run-down wheelchair had clung to the logs right through the beating without making a sound. When the rest of us had been yanked from the train the guard with the tiny moustache climbed onto the carriage. He grappled with Grandpa until the old man was sitting right on the edge of the carriage.

The guard spat in Grandpa's face.

'Kol Khara,' Grandpa said, *Eat shit.*

The man yelled, leapt forward and kicked the old man straight back off the train.

Grandpa's spine landed with a thump on the sharp rocks of the train track, he let out a soul-destroying scream. I leapt up and tried to drag him and his wheelchair away.

But the guards were ready for that. The tallest one swung his baton and a dull thud hit my shoulder. My arm transformed into a river of pain but I clung to the wheelchair and dragged him back while Mahdi and Jamal pushed at the men.

The men yelled, spat on us, and then walked back towards the carriage slapping each other on the back. I still held Grandpa in my hands. He was crying and the tears mixed with blood from a cut on his cheek.

In that moment I snapped from self-preservation to anger. I'd landed not far from an old fencepost.

I grabbed it and ran towards the train which had already begun to move off. I tried to catch up to the men who'd beat us. *You're going to pay.* I thought, *You cowards.*

But a sharp pain shot through my chest with every step. I was out of breath. I felt weak and the train was leaving me behind.

I turned on the passing carriages and whacked my stick against the train until it snapped on one of the wheels. I threw my stub at the final carriage and it bounced off with a small thud.

I shook my head as I fell to my bloody knees, *sometimes in life, there is no justice.*

****

Ayamin hugged me when I'd stumbled back to our raggedy, bloody group. Her head fitted into my shoulder and I can't remember exactly what she said but it was something about my anger, and how she loved it and how she loved me.

I hugged her tighter even though my chest hurt like hell, and then the two of us limped over to Grandpa who was being righted on his wheelchair by his two sons.

Mahdi looked up. He had the same anger in his eyes that I felt in my stomach. It was the anger of the powerless. We dropped our eyes as Mahdi's wife wiped the blood from Grandpa's face.

The kids were quiet.

Two of them held their mothers' hands, while the youngest stared in the direction the train had left.

'I don't like the conductors,' he sobbed.

We might have stayed there for hours, but a piercing whistle from another train came from the opposite direction. I looked at Ayamin, then I looked at Grandma. It seemed we all had the same idea.

We climbed the fence into a field of raggedy grass and large weeds and began to walk north, the way we'd been heading. The next field over was filled with pumpkins.

Wheezing. I stooped and picked one. Grandma was watching me. She picked one. Mahdi and Jamal picked a pumpkin each and Grandpa swore and swore and swore until Mahdi picked a small pumpkin for him to hold on his lap.

'Those pieces of shit,' he yelled as he bounced over the stems.

****

By the third day of our wandering, we weren't doing too well. One of the young boys and I were struggling to walk. My lungs felt hot and scratched as they moved against my ribs. The boy had a limp and a lemon sized lump on the side of his head.

But worst of all was Grandpa, he'd taken the fall from the train badly, and didn't have youth to aid his recovery. He'd bled from his nose and mouth four times, and moaned in his wheelchair as we moved. We had no pain relief, no access to a hospital, and didn't dare go too close to the railway line.

At around midday on the third day, we sat around eating slices of pumpkin we'd cooked over a fire and apples the kids and Aya had scavenged from a tree beside the railway line. Above us, thick concrete storm clouds crashed together and rain began to fall.

The drops were fat, fast, and increased in number rapidly.

At first, the cool water was welcoming. We could clean wounds properly and it numbed our bruises. But the torrent grew and grew until it was like standing under a fire hose.

With a flash of yellow, Ayamin pulled out our jacket and the two of us sheltered under it as we walked. Grandma and Mahdi's wife held a tarpaulin over Grandpa as he was wheeled along.

We passed through a waist-high stream that five minutes earlier would've been a trickle and when we reached the fields our feet began to sink into the mud.

We passed through a cow paddock, all the cows were cowering under two large trees and I thought about how much I'd like to do the same.

'We need shelter,' I shouted to the group. A moment later I slipped and landed hard on my chest. I felt my ribs bend and

I let out a scream of pain. The rain was deafening as it beat against the earth.

Ayamin eased her hands around my back. Trying to help as I squirmed to my feet. With a solid heave that left me breathless, I was standing. Ayamin's face came right up close to mine. Her hair was dripping and her eyes were dripping and her nose brushed mine.

'I was looking at that barn up ahead.' she shouted over the rain.

'Yeah. Barn good,' I shouted back.

We took two steps towards it, then I looked back, the rest of the family was with us apart from Grandma and Mahdi who were struggling to wheel and lift Grandpa through the mud.

Grandpa was moaning again, and his face had gone white with the pain of it. I felt something building in my chest. It felt like rage.

I handed our jacket to Ayamin, 'I'm just going to help wheel him over,' I said and began marching towards the old man.

My ribs gave little white-hot stabs of pain as I moved, but I think that only added to my rage. I reached the old man, yelled at Mahdi to pick up his side and together we lifted Grandpa off the ground.

The pain was out of this world. But the adrenaline it brought on was like a shot of morphine.

'Let's go,' I yelled at Mahdi and set off at a run.

My ribs hurt – they hurt like someone was twisting a screwdriver into them. But I just yelled all the harder. Ayamin watched me as I passed her, a big grin on her beautiful rain-streaked face.

'Go Danny, Go!' she yelled.

Grandpa was screaming, delirious with pain. But he had this wild grimace on his face. He could feel the same madness that had taken a hold of me.

'Go you animals! Run boys!'

Lightning flashed; thunder struck. I screamed into the rain all the swear words I'd ever learnt and when I ran out I just screamed like a wild lion. Everything was on fire and I could taste blood on my tongue.

We reached the barn – it had a gate in front but I made Mahdi jump over then half-threw Grandpa to him.

I stood in the rain panting with this wild smile on my face for about two seconds before my knees gave way and I was kneeling like a praying believer in the mud. I couldn't breathe. My lungs didn't seem to work.

Then I felt a hand on my back, a painful glance told me it was Grandma, 'That is good anger of yours boy,' she said.

Ayamin fell to her knees beside me. She was kissing me, all over my face. Over and over, the rain dripped down her hair.

'That was impressive,' she whispered.

I kissed her again and put my arms around her back, 'I think I got a little carried away.'

She laughed.

There were droplets of water on her face and I kissed them slowly. The two of us climbed over the gate and into the hay-barn. It was musty-dry inside but the hay smelt good and we all stripped out of our wet clothes.

As I moved my shoulder to take my t-shirt off my ribs screamed out in pain and I dropped my arm.

'Oh man,' I said, 'I'm starting to think the last five minutes were a bad idea.'

Ayamin laughed, and put her hands on my arm, 'You have the same look my Dad did, when he got angry there was nothing in this world that could stop him.'

She inched my arm upwards, 'Tell me when it hurts.'

I waited until the pain was getting close to unbearable. I liked the feel of her hands on my arm.

'There. It hurts there.'

She sucked in air between her teeth and winced, 'It looks like you finished what those guards started.'

Inch by inch Ayamin helped me ease my shirt off. I grinned at Mahdi who was receiving the same treatment from his wife.

'You'd make a good nurse,' I said as Ayamin tied my shirt into a sling.

'I hope you're not just saying that because I took your shirt off.'

'Well...' I grinned, 'No seriously, back in Turkey with the poppies for your grandmother and the other patients – you care.'

She tried to hide it but I could tell she was pleased, her hand dropped to my waist, 'Okay greaser, do you need nurse Ayamin to help you with the rest of your clothes?'

I raised an eyebrow, 'I mean, if you're offering...'

Next to me, Grandpa chuckled, 'This man is an opportunist,' Grandma started laughing and soon we all were, even the kids who didn't quite understand – they didn't care, it was laughter and we were safe and it felt good.

****

The hay was soft and slightly prickly to sleep on. But it was dry. I woke as light began to enter the hayshed and found a small piece of grass poking my cheek.

I yawned, stood up and walked over to where Ayamin and Grandma had started a little firepit near the entrance of the barn.

I sat down beside Ayamin and kissed her.

'How are you feeling Danny?'

I shrugged, 'Stiff and sore, but okay. I think the sleep helped.'

We sat watching the small flames lick at Grandma's pots.

While the storm raged outside it was relatively peaceful in the haybarn. It felt like maybe we were in the eye of the storm.

There was a sharp click of metal, and I looked around to see a thin, dark-bearded man wearing a dripping coat and pants standing in the entrance of the barn. He started shouting in Serbian and moving closer. In his hands was a soviet-looking rifle. It was pointed at us.

The rest of the family emerged from the hay like mice. Jamal helped Grandpa down into a sitting position.

We were sitting around the fire, Ayamin grabbed my hand, and Grandma's next to her. She nodded towards Mahdi's wife, and I took her hand. Within half a minute we were all linked and looking up at the gunman, waiting.

He seemed a little less sure of himself now. Like his plan had only gone this far.

He was moving from one foot to the other, and his jacket swayed from side to side. He shouted in Serbian again and waving his gun around. We all sat there with blank faces.

'English?' I tried.

The man snorted and continued his barrage of Serbian words. After about five minutes he seemed to run out of steam. The guy wasn't young. His hair was grey and his skin all wrinkled from a life outdoors.

In the pot oats and apples were boiling with a whistling sound. The Serbian pointed to the pot, said something in his language, then gestured with his hands like he was eating from a bowl.

Ayamin was the first to move. She reached slowly into a bag and pulled out a bowl and a spoon.

The man nodded.

Grandma scooped a heaped spoon of porridge, then a smaller spoon of the apple sauce. The Serbian man shouted, gestured for her to add another spoonful and then another.

One of the kids licked his tongue, looked up at the man, then back at our breakfast – now half gone. He could do the math.

The Serbian man took the bowl. With one hand on the trigger of the shotgun, he began eating and eating.

The man burped as he finished. Then smiled and pointed back to the bowl.

'I think he wants seconds,' Ayamin said.

'Pig' Grandma said in Arabic, but on her face, she wore a smile as she ladled more of the steaming meal into his bowl.

We watched him eat with desperate eyes. I saw the children whispering – *who was going to miss out?*

When the man had finished, he dumped the bowl back onto the hay and seemed unsure of his next move.

He sniffed, then pointed the gun at me, Mahdi, and Jamal then pointed out the door where the rain poured down.

I shrugged like I didn't understand, so he beckoned with his finger for us to follow, then with the gun still pointed at us he walked backwards into the rain.

We followed. Barefoot and all. Ayamin ran and grabbed our jacket – throwing it to me.

About fifty meters from the barn a faded orange car was bogged down in the mud. The angry man walked into the mud and mimed pushing it, then pointed at the three of us. I nodded as the rain beat down on us.

'Hey Mahdi, how you feeling man?' I asked.

'I'm good.'

'Well, my ribs hurt like hell. Think you guys have got it?'

Mahdi and Jamal looked at each other and gave a brothers' nod.

'Yeah we got it,' Jamal said.

They stood either side of the car, bending their knees like rugby players in a scrum. I stood in between them with my hands resting on the boot of the car. I hunched my shoulders slightly like I was ready to push but I just let my hands sit there. Little spiderwebs of pain spread out along my ribs. *What was I thinking yesterday?*

When he looked sure we wouldn't attack him the man jumped into the car, locked the doors, revved the engine, and stuck a hand out the window – pointing forwards.

My feet sunk into the cold mud and gravel below me. Gritty bits of sand rubbed against my ankles as the vehicle moved forward with both tires spinning.

After a minute-long fight, there was this sucking sound and the tyres began to move against the gravel. The car shot out of its place and the Serbian man gave two toots of the horn.

The man got out of his car, leaving the gun on the front seat, but armed himself with a large sack of potatoes. He handed them to us, then pulled three oranges from a small bag in his back seat.

He gave one to each of us which we accepted like men who'd won the lottery.

The man said something in Serbian, winked, and jumped in his car.

As the faded orange car sped along a track towards an old rickety house in the distance, I looked at Mahdi, and then Jamal. The brothers' eyebrows were wrinkled – they were confused, and so was I.

****

Back at the barn the oranges were cut up and passed around. The kids weren't quite so angry about being cheated out of half their breakfast after that.

When everyone had eaten, there was a big debate about what to do next.

Mahdi was all for going.

'If that idiot shoots one of us – or calls the police we're done.'

His wife was nodding her head, one kid sat on her knee, his head bobbed up and down as her knee shook, the kid didn't seem to mind though. Bits of the orange were smeared around his mouth and he was licking at the peels.

But beside her, Grandma wasn't so sure.

'You look out there, you see the rain. Grandpa will never survive, the kids too. If they get cold there'll be nowhere to recover. We need to leave *yes*. But we can't leave in rain like this.'

In the end, Grandma won. We stayed another night – filling ourselves up with baked potatoes throughout the day.

By the next morning, the rain had eased. As it grew light, we began to pack. But just as we were pulling our bags onto our backs a steady clattering of metal interrupted us.

The Serbian man had returned. Only this time he carried four shovels instead of a gun. He carefully laid the shovels down outside the haybarn, then pulled a few Serbian banknotes from his pocket.

He laid the money – two notes with 500 written on them on the ground, then stared at us with an almost pleading look in his eyes.

'How much do you think that is?' I whispered to Ayamin.

'Not much,' she said, 'He doesn't look rich.'

'Should we take it?'

She shrugged and looked at Grandma, as the rest of the family was doing. The old woman had a hand resting on her chin as she stared at the tools and money in front of her.

The Serbian seemed to realise that the ultimate power lay with her and he held up his hands, running back to his car.

Five minutes later he returned with three cartons of eggs and milk in a steel bucket. He opened each tray of eggs so they faced us, but I hardly noticed. I was too fixated on the frothy milk in the bucket. It felt like years since I'd tasted that creamy goodness.

Grandma raised her eyebrows but didn't nod yes or no. With a grin, the man produced two tomatoes from his jacket and laid them down beside the eggs. He folded his arms and we all stared at Grandma.

'Danny, Ayamin, how do you feel about working?' she asked without turning her head.

I shrugged, 'My ribs are stuffed, but my stomach has the final say.'

Grandma nodded to me, then turned and nodded to the Serbian. A smile filled his face.

We sat in a circle and passed around the stainless-steel bucket with milk in it while the Serbian farmer watched. The taste was unreal – almost like honey, but cooler and softer. A thick layer of cream had settled on top and I swallowed three gulps before passing it on to Mahdi.

The Serbian took us to the edge of a field and showed us how to dig holes for fence posts. We worked most of the day and then when we'd finished the Serbian came back and sat down to eat with us.

While the kids gave him a few strange looks, Grandma acted as if nothing was different. She gave him the first serving, and we watched with pained eyes as he wolfed it down. When he reached for more Grandma shook her head and replaced the lid.

'No.'

The farmer shifted his hand away and watched as she served the kids, Grandpa, and finally herself. The pan was empty and his face had gone a bright red. He put down his bowl and stormed out of the barn.

'Mister Farmer is coming back with his rifle,' Mahdi said.

His wife shook her head, 'Mister Farmer's coming back with the police.'

Their youngest kid sat between them, clutching his mum and shivering with wide eyes, 'He's going to bring the train conductors.'

It was almost dark when the farmer returned. He lugged a big brown sack on his back that almost made him sink into the mud.

Mahdi and I stood as the man approached the barn. He stood like a silhouette in the doorway – half Boogieman and half Santa Claus.

He walked inside and upended the sack onto the hay in front of Grandma.

Bread, apples, carrots, flour, oranges, spaghetti, tinned apricots, potatoes, biscuits, and lollies spilled in front of us. The kids' mouths fell open. Little piles of drool landed on the hay.

But that wasn't our biggest surprise – the farmer said a word – not in his language, or even English. He spoke in Arabic... and he said 'Eat.'

'Eat, eat, eat, eat, eat.'

****

A month later and we were still with the Serbian. We had a stockpile of Serbian notes, our chests were filling out again, and our hands had grown calloused from digging posts, milking cows, and putting in a massive vegetable garden.

I was enjoying myself – I'd begun to learn Serbian, I got to spend solid time just being with Ayamin rather than surviving with her, and the farm work suited me. My ribs were healing and I felt strong and well.

But Ayamin had feet that itched for the road, and eyes that longed for England. I could see it in the way she gazed off into the horizon, or the way she went quiet when Grandma talked about settling down.

It was on a clear night while sitting under the canopy of an ancient tree that she told me she couldn't take farm life anymore.

'I want an education Danny, and I want to build a life in England.'

I just nodded. I didn't have to say I'd follow her, she already knew that 'I'll miss Mahdi and the kids,' I said, 'and Grandma – she'll miss you too you know.'

'But they're building a life for themselves,' she said, 'we need to do the same.'

I looked up at the stars and suddenly I was hit by a feeling – it was close to loneliness. All this talk of building lives made me think about my lack of future.

When I got to England, I'd be in a bit of a pickle – I'd have to make a false identity or go to jail neither of which would be practical for whatever comes next with Ayamin.

I reached out for her hand. It was warm, but the warmth didn't seem to make a difference. I considered telling her about it all – the real reason I'd gone to Turkey. About court, and prison, and breaking into the stores. It would have to happen at some stage, and under that night sky would've been perfect.

But I shrugged it off – told myself to worry about it later, just focus on the moment because I was enjoying the moment. I stared up at the sky then reached out to run my hand along Ayamin's leg.

She broke her intense meditative stare-off with the sky and smiled with a mischievous sideways glance.

She rolled over until her face was inches from mine. Her breath tickled my neck as she whispered,

'Feeling playful?'

My body stiffened but my hands knew what they wanted, they reached for her hips and pulled her on top of me. I kissed her and it lasted a long hot minute before she reached under my shirt and traced her nail along my sides. There were lights in her eyes.

That was... a good night.

****

In the morning I was woken by a distant sobbing. It sounded old and heartbroken. It was Grandma.

I slipped out from beside Ayamin and ran to the barn. Inside, the family was sitting around Grandpa, who lay back in the hay the same way he'd slept the night before – only now his face was blue and his chest had stopped moving. When I touched his hand it was stone cold.

With the help of the farmer, we moved him to a small patch of grass under an old oak tree and placed him in the soft earth beneath it. For the first time since I'd met her, Grandma didn't look strong or in control, her hand trembled in mine.

Much later as the sun was setting, I looked out from the barn to see her lone silhouette shivering in front of the tree.

It was two weeks later that Ayamin and I finally decided to leave the camp. Hugging the family as we left was too much for us. First I started to cry, and then Ayamin couldn't help herself. Opposite me, Mahdi wiped at tears of his own.

'Danny brother,' he said, 'This is not goodbye – you make sure you come back. I think Mister Farmer would be very happy if you brought a shovel too.'

We both laughed, and I hugged him again.

They'd decided to stay, the work was okay and 'Mister Farmer' had arranged for the kids to be enrolled in a school.

Grandma was the last one waiting to say goodbye to us. She'd become thin since Grandpa had left, but some of her spirit was beginning to return.

As we stepped away from the hug Grandma held us with her arms. She placed a hand on each of our foreheads and began to sing a prayer in Arabic. I couldn't catch the words but the sound was happy-sad.

When she stepped away, she stared at us with her big brown eyes.

'This means you are family. You will always have people to call home.'

I opened my mouth to say something in return. But the words wouldn't come. Instead, I wrapped my arms around the woman once more and hugged her until I was sure she'd never fade from me.

Then I pulled the pack onto my back and took Ayamin's hand.

'Goodbye family.' Grandma said.

'Goodbye family,' Ayamin and I repeated.

And we began to walk down the dirt track to the farm gate.

****

It was a strange feeling only being the two of us. Our footsteps on the metal road sounded hollow compared to how they'd sounded as a group.

We took the wrong turn initially and ended up in a village slightly south of the farm. By the time we'd retraced our footsteps darkness was falling. We walked a little further, then found a strand of scraggly trees to disappear under.

Ayamin brushed the Winnie the Pooh tent as we unpacked him. There were fade marks from where he'd been folded.

'At least you'll be happy Mr Winnie,' she said, 'It's been a while since you've seen the moonlight.'

That night I was woken by every rustle, cough, or vehicle that came by us. The ground underneath me was hard and lumpy compared to the sweet-smelling hay we'd been sleeping on.

I rolled over onto my side for the millionth time, trying to find a comfortable spot, 'Life on the road,' I whispered to myself, 'Isn't all it's cracked up to be.'

'You're awake too?' whispered Ayamin from next to me.

'Just sleep talking,' I moaned, 'How could anyone be awake after sleeping on this plush soft ground.'

Out of the corner of my eye, I saw her smile.

'Well, I'm glad you're enjoying it. I was going to cuddle, but if you're sleeping, I won't disturb you.'

'Are you sure?'

She laughed, 'No, I'd hate to wake you.'

I was silent for a moment, then let out a loud yawn and stretched out my arms, 'Ahhh... that was such a good sleep.'

'So, you're awake now?'

'Yep, and what a refreshing sleep that was.'

She giggled and rolled over to my side of the mattress.

I wish I could remember the number of days it took us to pass through Serbia, but I can't. The setting up and taking down of Winnie the Pooh blended into one another and after a while each mile felt the same for our tired feet.

That is until we reached the fence.

****

At first glance, Hungary looked like a hedgehog. We arrived just before dawn and the part of Hungary's border we'd stumbled upon was protected by a high-tech security fence with wire and antennas and cameras dotted along it like spikes. Speakers shouted warnings at us in at least five languages, including English and Arabic.

'East or West?' I asked Ayamin.

She glanced both ways along the fence, 'Let's go West.'

So we turned and started walking along the fence, glancing at the solid wire mesh, trying to find a way through.

After half a mile we spotted an old Hungarian man crouched on his side of the fence with a pair of gardening shears. He was whistling to himself as he cut the wires. When he saw us he gave a wave.

'Hello there,' he said in heavily accented Arabic.

We were both too confused to speak. I wondered if we were so exhausted that we were seeing visions. But... the old man remained.

He'd cut two wires and bent them back to create a small hole. The man had been lining up a third wire when he'd spotted us.

He waved for us to come over. Ayamin and I glanced at each other and... limped over to where he crouched.

'The trouble is,' he explained, 'They keep using thicker and thicker wire. Soon it'll be so thick I'll need a hacksaw,' he shuddered, 'Those things aren't cheap if you're unemployed.'

He placed the shears either side of the wire and squeezed down on them, twisting slightly as he went. He was bundled up in a worn winter jacket and a woollen hat. The effort of cutting the wire made him sweat.

'Do you want help?' I asked, reaching for the shears.

'No!' He pulled them away. Ayamin and I froze. The man wiped at his forehead, 'If they catch you, you will be thrown in the prison.'

He watched us until he was sure I wouldn't try to take the shears, then he went back to cutting the wire. The shears wiggled back and forth.

'What about you?' I asked, 'Won't you go to jail?'

'They wouldn't dare,' he said, beginning to sweat again, 'I'm the king you see.'

'Of Hungary?' Ayamin asked.

The man gave one last twist and the wire snapped. He nodded to Ayamin, 'I am the king of Hungary, welcome to my country,' he bent the cut wires back towards him then gestured for us to climb through.

Ayamin looked at me, *should we?* she mouthed.

I glanced from her to the maniac-king on the other side of the fence. He was drinking something alcoholic from a flask, there was dirt on his hands and knees from kneeling to cut the wire. I looked back at Ayamin and shrugged.

She climbed through the hole and I followed.

As we stood brushing the dust off our knees the King of Hungary started to walk off towards the sunrise, carrying his garden shears like a sword, and wearing his holey woollen hat like a crown.

'Hey,' I called.

The man stopped and turned.

'Thank you.'

A little smile appeared on his lips, 'Just doing my job.'

I reached into the bag for the final two apples we'd taken from a tree in Serbia as the king disappeared from view.

I passed the bigger apple to Ayamin, 'This'll be our last meal for a while.'

She nodded to me, took a bite, winced, then rubbed her eyes and started walking north, away from the border. I followed her, taking a bite of my apple.

It was mushy and not very sweet but I forced it down, seeds and all.

After an hour's walk, we met a road that linked with a major highway. The sun was well up by now and as it bounced off the clouds, cast a golden-grey reflection over the land.

****

I woke far too early on our second day in Hungary. The stomach pain I thought I'd escaped the night before returned with a vengeance. I lay awake for a few hours before Ayamin started to toss and turn.

The tent felt too hot and sticky, she rolled over to me.

'Are you asleep Danny?'

'No. I'm starving.'

'Stop thinking about it then. It makes things worse.'

I tried to stop thinking about it... I tried to focus on how my arms felt, on the sounds of birds rustling about, on Ayamin's breath as it brushed my face. But then my stomach gave a big rumble and the gnawing hunger returned.

'Ayamin are you hungry?'

'Yes.'

'Stop thinking about it... Just think about this beautiful country that we're in.'

'Danny, we're in Hungary.'

'Exactly,' I laughed, before clutching my stomach again, 'We are hungry in Hungary.'

Ayamin shook her head, but she laughed, she laughed a good long while, 'You are so lame...'

'I know... but it did take your mind off your stomach didn't it?'

'I guess.'

There was a moment of silence before Ayamin turned to me.

'Danny, I'm hungry in Hungary.'

We cracked up laughing. We kept laughing until I felt tears in my eyes and my jaw was getting sore. I tried to breathe, but then I looked at Ayamin and I started all over again.

It felt good.

Eventually, we crawled out of the tent and lay on the grass looking at the sky.

'We've come a long way,' Ayamin said, 'I think maybe we should rest when we get to Budapest.'

'And eat,' I said, pulling up my shirt to expose my lean ribs, 'And eat and eat and eat until we're so fat we'll have to roll to England.'

Ayamin laughed, 'Actually, you're pretty fit Danny,' she ran her hand across my stomach, 'Mr six-pack.'

'I'd trade my six-pack for fish and chips,' I said, closing my eyes, and rubbing her hand where it sat on my stomach, 'Salt, a crunchy batter, white fish, steaming fries, and a squeeze of lemon. God, there's nothing more beautiful in this world,' I paused for a moment, then opened one eye and glanced at Ayamin, 'Well... except you of course.'

Ayamin clutched at her heart, 'Did you really just call me more beautiful than fish and chips?'

I laughed, 'And I meant every word of it.'

She shook her head in wonder, 'Danny, you really know what to say to a girl.'

****

That day we walked on empty stomachs. I was light-headed, and when the meagre sun came out from behind a bank of cheeseburger-shaped-clouds, I thought I'd pass out. Imagine a hangover, but there's no food in the fridge.

We passed several towns, but most of them were too small – or the locals too hostile for us to try scavenge for something.

Every few steps my right foot would start to drag on the ground. At nightfall, I turned to Ayamin.

'I know I'm not going to sleep like this.'

'Me either,' she said.

'I was thinking we should just keep walking into the night.'

She yawned... and looked down at her feet.

'Yeah, why not.'

The two of us plodded on until the moon was high in the sky and we were getting wobbly on our feet. Then we stumbled off the road into a small area of woodland and slept under an old elm tree.

We woke feeling sick and hungry at the same time. I was having visions of all the food I'd ever wasted including a cheese toastie that I'd let drop on the floor.

The memory of that cheese toastie had a real impact on my muddled mind. As we got up to leave, I felt tears roll down my cheeks.

'What's wrong?' Ayamin asked.

'You wouldn't understand...' I said as I tried to squeeze the tears out.

'Oh Danny,' she wrapped her arms around me, hugged me and rubbed circles on my back, 'Tell me what's wrong.'

'It's stupid.'

'No, come on.'

I sniffed, 'Okay so back in England this one time **sniff** I'd made the best cheese toastie you've ever seen, cheese heaped all over it, this beautiful pickle, ham. **sniff** My god it was to die for, and then it drops off my plate and falls onto the dirt,' I clung to Ayamin, weeping into her shoulder, 'I threw it away. God, what an idiot.'

Ayamin laughed, then clutched her stomach, 'I was thinking about Teete's spicy chicken and chickpea.'

We hugged tight, then clutched our stomachs and talked about food as we shuffled our way along.

Reminiscing about food probably wasn't the best idea, but by that point, our self-control was too weak for anything else.

We found a small stream and drank as much water as we could. But water is like air. It can't fill your stomach. It sort of just sloshed around inside of us.

On that third day, and nearly fainting with hunger, the two of us stumbled into first the suburbs and then the heart of Budapest.

And that's where we stopped.

****

Morning. The sun crawled through the streets searching for us, maybe hoping to give us some courage. It wouldn't have found us. Ayamin and I lay curled under a bridge, our blanket tossed over us.

Ayamin had shivered all night, even with our bodies pressed together. It wasn't until dawn approached that I realised I was shivering too. When she looked at me in the morning her eyes were rings of black.

'You look like a panda,' she told me.

The two of us crawled from under our bridge and began walking the streets. Movement and the sun helped to warm us. We passed by coffee shops and breakfast places, holding our stomachs as we forced ourselves to keep moving. Food was plentiful, but not for us.

We stopped outside a McDonalds and I spotted two nearly full rubbish bins. I nodded to Aya, 'I'll get us something.'

I checked both ways for some sort of police officer, then bent next to the bin and began pulling out half-eaten hash browns, chips, and striking gold, even a happy meal with some apple slices and chicken nuggets.

I carried our feast back to Ayamin. We walked to the stone steps of a church, a little way away from the McDonalds and sat down with it.

She stared at the half-eaten cheeseburger and slightly old fries. It shows just how hungry she was when she began to tear into the cheeseburger.

Parts of the happy meal were still warm and we ate the apple pieces for 'dessert'. When the food had finished, I went back for more. We repeated the process three times. As I was going for a fourth Ayamin stopped me.

'We're gonna be sick.'

With a full stomach, I found that I could think once more. And I felt so damn happy. Like I was floating on a cloud of bliss.

I gazed around, eyeing up landmarks and trying to figure out our next move. Ayamin took my hand.

'Hey, we're in Budapest...' she said, 'People dream of coming here. Let's pretend just for a bit like we're on holiday.'

So we did. We sat there and we watched Budapest come to life in the morning sun. Chains of kids and parents passed by on their way to school. People in suits passed men who stood outside their shops smoking. A group of fruit and vegetable sellers set up shop near us and were soon enveloped by hordes of restaurateurs and couples.

After watching a while, we decided to tour the city. We followed the promenade along the edge of the Danube River. As we walked, I spotted a brown, wide-brimmed hat with a feather in it leaning against a rubbish bin. I put the feathered hat on and held out my arm to Ayamin. She slipped hers through mine and soon we were touring the city like a royal couple.

'We should come back and visit these places someday,' I said, 'I'll get a job when we're back in England, save money so that we can go on fancy cruises and eat whenever we want.'

She smiled. Below us, small waves lapped the shore as a tour boat passed by. We stood there, just watching it.

Most of the people on board wore white. I saw old people with cameras, middle-aged businesspeople reading books, and a girl and a guy about our age lying on lounge chairs scrolling through their phones.

Something about the couple made me keep staring at them. They were arguing... she flipped him the middle finger, his face was going red. He stood up, moved to her chair and grabbed her shoulders.

For a moment both their faces were turned towards us. Their clean faces with furrowed brows and snarling lips, and then the boat turned and they were gone.

I looked over at Ayamin. She was still watching the boat. I lifted my thumb to the side of her face and traced a thin line in the layer of dust that coated it.

She turned to me, 'I'm a pretty simple girl Danny, if we ever come back, let's take a van... you know just put a mattress in the back to sleep on.'

The two of us found a public garden, lay down and slept on the grass for a few hours under the warm sun. After that, we had an early dinner at one of the finest restaurants on the left side of the Danube river.

By that I mean Ayamin kept watch while I jumped into the restaurant's large garbage bin and pulled out anything that looked fresh.

I ended up smelling rather rotten, but hey, for once I was earning my keep.

We had salmon, a fancy Greek salad, and even a mouth-watering steak!

After dinner, we swam in the Danube and sunbathed in the sun's dying light. As orange and purple hues filled the sky we returned to our five-star accommodation under one of Budapest's many bridges.

'Hey Danny,' Ayamin said, her hair tumbled over my chest as she rested, and her eyes were reflecting the dying sun, 'This is bliss.'

Slowly I ran my hand through her hair, 'But you're sleeping under a bridge, ate food from the garbage, and had to bathe in a slightly polluted river... Are you out of your mind??'

She laughed, then dragged her hand across my chest, I wrapped my arms around her.

'Us meeting must've been fate,' she said, running her thumb across my cheek, 'If you didn't have your Red Cross mission or I'd left the camp earlier, none of this would've happened.'

I nodded, 'It's crazy that the greatest moments of your life appear out of nowhere. You can't pick them looking forwards, only looking back.'

Ayamin kissed my lips. We had full bellies, it was a starry sky. We were poor, refugees, but in that moment, everything felt just right.

****

We woke. It had been raining and the two of us huddled together under the bridge. Ayamin shivered as she tried to nestle in closer to me.

We watched the sun attempt to break through the rain clouds. The fight lasted maybe half an hour but eventually, the rain clouds had it swamped. It was going to be a grey day.

Putting our blanket in the bag, and snacking on a little bread from the night before, we began to move. Autumn was quickly turning into winter, and I watched Ayamin as she rubbed her feet before putting them into her boots. We wouldn't survive well in a winter here.

'We should look at moving,' Ayamin said as we walked through town. The buildings appeared greyer than the day before, and people were bundled up in coats of black and grey.

Ayamin was wearing our yellow jacket, I wore a red sweat-shirt I'd found and it was almost as if we were the only objects of colour in the city.

'Do you think someone here would let me work for them?' I thought aloud, looking at signs in shop windows.

She shrugged, 'I read an article once about refugees who work for days, then when they come for their pay the boss just calls the cops.'

'So what do we do?' I asked, 'Beg?'

'Maybe? I'm sure we'd fit in.'

I rubbed the side of my head, three people were begging in the alleyway in front of us and they were all wearing nicer clothes than ours.

'Let's do it,' I said with a shrug... 'Doesn't look like we have too many other options.'

For breakfast, we ate some half-eaten food we'd found outside a restaurant. Then the two of us found ourselves a wide alleyway with plenty of people passing through. There was only one other beggar in sight – a tanned, wrinkled old man leaning against a guitar. We figured we weren't stepping in anyone's territory.

As we sat, I looked at Ayamin. I'd heard of some people dressing rough to get more money, but Ayamin didn't need to do that.

Her jacket and pants, stained and torn in various places hung from her body. Her face had a sleek angular look that would've made a few of the girls back home in England pretty jealous, but Ayamin's look also had a hardness to it.

'What are you staring at?' she said.

'A skinny street rat.'

She laughed, 'Come on, let's just give begging a go, we only need enough for a bus to the border.'

A businessman was walking towards us, the phone in his hands would've been worth enough to get us to England. We held out our hands, trying to look as sorry as we could.

He passed by without a glance, the clip of his shoes slowly receded down the stones of the alleyway towards the man with the guitar. I looked at Ayamin, she just shrugged and held her hands out as a group moved down the alley.

By midday, we had the equivalent of one British pound and Ayamin decided it was time for a lunch break.

'At this rate, we're going to be here a month just to get to the border,' I said as we dug into some half-eaten pastries.

Ayamin shook her head, 'I could go for a hotel room and a hot shower right about now.'

We spent the rest of the day at 'work' holding our hands out and hoping someone would be generous enough to drop something into them. The whole time we were there, the guitar man lying just down from us didn't play his guitar once, he sort of had it leaned up against him as he slouched, probably drunk, against the wall behind him.

When the streetlights came on we made our way back to the bridge we'd been sleeping under. I counted the coins and notes with a faint click. It was less than two pounds worth. As our footsteps knocked on the concrete we heard voices coming from the bridge. Moving a little closer we saw a group of four young guys dressed in rags similar to ours gathered around a candle. They were heating a broken lightbulb with sticky black heroin inside of it. One of them primed a vein on his arm, while another drew the molten liquid into a long syringe.

'Let's go,' Ayamin whispered, taking my hand.

We moved away from the bridge, and I held her hand a little tighter. Ayamin might have torn clothes and unwashed hair, but in my opinion, she was still way too pretty to spend a night out in the open.

The streetlights came on, giving us light, but doing nothing to help us find a place to stay. Ayamin squeezed my hand as she walked.

'It's okay Danny,' she said, 'It's okay.'

'I know, but it's dangerous for both of us.'

Ayamin stopped as we heard a drunken Hungarian shout from behind us.

'Keep walking,' I whispered. Ayamin stared straight ahead as we picked up our speed a little. The shout came again, almost bearlike. Ayamin's breathing came loud as the drunk ran towards us.

'Oiiii,' the man yelled from no more than two meters behind us. I turned; it was instinct. You never leave your back unprotected.

We were faced by a large man with a small moustache. I stepped forward and put my arm around Ayamin, the man's gaze swept her tattered clothes.

His eyes shifted from her to me. I gazed around for a cop or some sort of saviour. There was no one.

The man grinned at me but it was all teeth. I raised my hands and balled them into fists. I'd met assholes like this in England. If you gave them an inch, they'd walk right over you. I just wished I had a steel pole or something to make it a little more even.

Drunken dude grinned; it was probably a two for one deal for him. He'd get to fight, then carry away the refugee girl. He held up his fists, I spotted a broken nose between them. He must've been some sort of a boxer.

The man spat something in Hungarian then moved towards me, meaty ham-fists raised. I wasn't going to fight properly with Ayamin on the line so I brought my foot up in a quick arc that ended in his balls.

Drunk dude let out a groan and I stepped closer, poking him in the eyes twice, then punching him in the nose.

His big ham-fist swung out and caught me on the side of my head, I heard Aya scream and another fist hit my chest, the air rushed out of my lungs and I bent in half.

A brick hit the man's shoulder and I caught a glimpse of Ayamin about to hurl a bottle. My chest wheezed as I hit the man in the nose again.

But his skull must've been too thick for the pain to have an effect. He grabbed me by the shirt as I hit him over and over again. His large fist twisted and dumped me to the ground. I felt my mind go black for a moment, then a dizzy sensation swept through me as I watched the man walk towards Ayamin. I struggled to my feet, vomit forming in my throat. Ayamin was yelling something in Arabic, the man didn't seem to care.

Then there was another voice. A dry, calm voice that spoke two words in Hungarian. The big thug slowed to a standstill, then turned. Silhouetted in the streetlights was an older man dressed in rags with weather-beaten skin wrinkled by age.

The drunk man shouted at him, then spat in his direction. The old guy didn't move. He didn't sway. He just stood there staring, like a marble statue.

The big Hungarian waved his arms and turned back towards Ayamin. Bending down the old guy picked up the brick Aya had thrown. He said a sentence in Hungarian, his tone calm and commanding. The drunk man froze. His face reared into a hideous snarl, then he turned and limped off.

The old man waited until the drunk man had disappeared around a corner before he dropped the brick. The moment it hit the ground, time seemed to unfreeze, and my head began to throb again. Ayamin let out a sob and I felt her hands on me, trying to help me to my feet.

The man who'd saved us just turned and walked away.

'It's okay, it's okay,' Ayamin said as she lifted me. A slight breeze was passing us by and it made me stagger like I was the drunk.

Ayamin held my head between her hands, 'How do you feel Danny?' she said, 'How many fingers am I holding up?'

I blinked, then tried to focus, behind her the man who'd saved us was watching, Ayamin waved her fingers in front of me, 'Two,' I said, 'You're holding two.'

She kissed my forehead. 'You were so brave Danny.'

I coughed, my head felt like cracked eggshells, 'Actually, the brave one is standing just over there.'

With our eyes on him, the old man who'd saved us shouted something in Hungarian and waved his hands like he wanted to get rid of us. He picked up a guitar that was leaning up against a wall and strode over to the alleyway we'd been begging in earlier.

Ayamin and I didn't move. I was having trouble making a plan. I knew we couldn't go back to our bridge, but my ideas kept disappearing into the murky soup that had become my mind.

I felt Aya's hand rubbing my back, 'It's okay,' she said, 'There, there,' she helped me to stumble forward and I felt my head begin to clear a little.

On the other side of the street, people laughed and stumbled as they left a club. I remember seeing a woman looking in our direction, but no one came over to us. As we stumbled past the alleyway, I heard the old man's rumbly voice.

He stood there shaking his head like he was sorry we existed, he let out a sigh and waved his hand for us to follow him.

I looked to Ayamin to make a decision, I felt we could trust him, but then again, my head was scrambled.

Ayamin nodded with her big brown eyes and the two of us limped into the alleyway after him.

****

It turns out that the man who'd saved us was the same busker we'd seen earlier in the day. He carried his guitar case and a rucksack to a small overhang on the edge of a building and gestured with a quick roll of his eyes for us to sit down.

Ayamin helped me crawl into the space which smelled faintly of drugs and pigeons. It felt good to sit, yet at the same time, I felt my headache increasing. I laid my head against the cold concrete wall as Ayamin pulled a blanket from the pack.

The old man sat opposite us, cross-legged. He pulled a small resealable bag from his rucksack and proceeded to roll a joint. Ayamin and I watched in silence. When he finished, he lit it, took a puff, then offered it to me.

Ayamin shook her head, 'No, no,' but the man just stretched a little further.

'Ma, ma... madicine,' he said, touching his head, 'Pain.'

Gently I took the weed from him. Ayamin watched, her eyes so wide they almost covered her whole face. I took a slow draw on the joint. It reminded me of my time in high school.

After a few puffs, I began to feel the weed clouding my mind even further. Only this time it was a comforting cloud-like mist that hugs the land and makes it feel warm and protected.

I handed the joint back to the old man who offered it to Ayamin. She stared at the joint for a moment before taking it awkwardly in her hand. Gently she sucked in the smoke and as she tried to exhale, she coughed. The old man and I laughed.

Ayamin handed back the joint with a red face, 'This is a crazy night,' she whispered.

I grinned and rested my head against her. After a few more hits I felt so relaxed and so tired at the same time. We pushed the pack and our jacket behind us and used them as a pillow.

I looked at the old man, he'd extinguished the joint and was now in a similar position to us, gazing up at the sky.

'Thank you.' I said, with a bow of my head.

The man just sniffed, then spat out of the entrance and murmured something vaguely Hungarian.

I felt Ayamin's hand on my tender shoulder and I gently laid my arm over her. The weed and concussion combined to send me into a very deep sleep.

****

Morning came. I felt groggy, but I'd survived the night. I opened my eyes just slightly. The sun was beginning to shine down on us and Ayamin sat next to me, staring out into the street.

'You awake Danny?' she asked as I shifted around.

I tried to open my eyes a little further, the daylight was almost blinding, 'That was the longest sleep of my life.'

Ayamin still had a few rings around her eyes, but they seemed smaller than before. 'I couldn't wake you.'

With a hearty groan, I sat up. Aside from a few cigarette butts, the other side of the overhang was empty.

'He's working,' Ayamin said, holding up her hand, 'Just listen a moment.'

We both stopped, and slowly my ears began to pick up a familiar tune.

'It's Bob Dylan,' I said, '*Blowin' in the Wind.*'

We sat listening, watching the people go by. Ayamin had found leftover burgers from the night before so hunger was far from our minds. It was peaceful.

As the sun rose, we shifted out onto the street. We passed the old man strumming his guitar, 'Good morning,' I said.

He just nodded and kept strumming.

We sat on our jacket, held our hands out, and waited to see what the day would bring. I could see the old man watching us and shaking his head as he strummed.

By midday, we had the equivalent of half a pound. The old man walked over to us and stood with his hands on his hips. He shook his head. 'Nem.'

We watched as he pointed to the guitar case he'd had in front of him. It was half-full with coins. He reached into the bin near us and pulled out a coffee cup. After washing it under a dripping pipe he sat the cup in front of us, then left back to his guitar without a word.

In the next two hours, we made more money than we had the previous day. It was like the little coins and notes needed someplace to rest.

Towards the end of the day, we collected our jingling cup of coins, found two boxes of half-eaten pizzas, then walked over to our new friend to celebrate.

The old man sat counting his riches, with his guitar he'd managed to make far more than we had, probably enough to last him the week. He nodded at us and took a slice of pizza.

That night the three of us gathered in his little den and ate. The man poked holes in the bottom of a small tin, put pieces of wood and paper inside, then lit it. Pretty soon our little nook had a little fire. Ayamin held my hand and rubbed the back of it with her thumb. Opposite us, the man pulled out his guitar. He placed a calloused finger to the string, then stared up into space for a moment.

He began with Hobo's Lullaby. Mashing the English words to make it sound like a cry. His voice suited the song. Old and gravelly. I felt like I was on a train with him.

Do not think 'bout tomorrow
Let tomorrow come and go
Tonight you're in a nice warm boxcar
Safe from all that wind and snow...

****

The old man's song was still ringing in my ears a week later when I found a way for us to keep moving.

We'd almost saved up enough to get us on a bus to Vienna, but Ayamin wanted a little more money for when we got there.

'We're safe at the moment,' she said, 'and winter is coming.'

We'd felt it in our bones when we sat on the hard-cold street. Rainclouds meant two days had been spent begging under a roof. We made next to nothing, but couldn't afford to stop.

Other than begging and listening to our new friend play his guitar, our time was spent travelling the city. We explored everything that was free and open to us and a couple of places that weren't. It was on one of these trips that we passed a CCD Bank.

The bank was made of big white stone shaped into gothic spirals and pillars. Its entrance was gaping, like a giant eating all the mortals that stepped into it.

I turned, stared at Ayamin with her knotty black hair and face gone pale from the cold. I pointed at the bank.

'I think I might know how to get some money.'

Ayamin shook her head, throwing the cardboard crust of a three-day-old pizza into the bin, 'You can't rob a bank Danny.'

'I don't want to rob a bank.... I want to rob myself. I had an account there with maybe two hundred pounds in it.'

The two of us stood outside the bank for an hour discussing the best way to get money out. I had no card to withdraw it and as Ayamin pointed out, my clothes and hair were very hobo-like.

'I think,' she said, attempting her best snooty Paris fashion designer impression, 'I think what you need is a makeover.'

I laughed until she grabbed my hand and dragged me in the direction of a clothing shop, we peered through the windows of five of them before we came to a christian second-hand store with big crosses either side of the doorway and rows of slightly stained fabrics heaped together on racks.

We pushed open the door and went inside, 'How are we going to buy anything?' I whispered, eyeing up the labels.

'We're not,' she said, 'Or at least I hope not.'

Two women were manning the shop front. A middle-aged Hungarian and an elderly woman with Syrian features and a distinct grandmother look about her, like at any moment she'd pop up with a tray of biscuits still hot from the oven.

Ayamin approached the grandmother.

'Excuse me miss,' she said in Arabic, lowering her voice, 'My friend and I are looking for some clothes.'

The woman smiled at the language and looked both of us up and down, 'I can see that my dears, what's your budget?'

Ayamin blushed and held out a single note which wouldn't have covered buying a pair of second-hand socks.

The woman stared at it for a moment then nodded, 'We'll see what we can do with that.'

I gazed across at the younger woman who was staring at us. She said something in Hungarian, which the lady helping us completely ignored.

'Come along kids,' the woman said in Arabic.

I smiled, 'Thank you.'

'He's got a big appointment,' Ayamin explained, 'I thought I'd better dress him up a bit.'

'A job?' the woman asked.

'He's going to see the bank.'

The woman nodded like she'd been given an enormous task, 'Okay, but you also want something that you can travel in, right? A suit wouldn't be practical.'

Ayamin nodded, 'Yeah something light, that won't be worn through next week. Also, the colour green suits his eyes...'

They both laughed, the woman held a shirt up next to me and Aya inspected it critically. I felt like some Hollywood star on his way to a red-carpet event.

'Oh man you are going to look so good in these,' Ayamin held up some rough wearing chinos. The woman handed me a different shirt, with a semi-jacket to go over it.

As I changed Ayamin and the woman chatted, their voices were cut short by a harsh Hungarian voice. I quickly buttoned up the jacket and emerged just as the other storekeeper was leaving with her fists balled up.

'What'd she want?' I asked.

The older woman shook her head, 'She told me not to speak in Arabic, and to stop looking after *my own people*.'

Ayamin and I stared as the older woman shrugged, 'But if we don't help ourselves who will? We're not getting much love from anybody else.'

She turned back to my outfit and nodded, 'Anyway, I think my job here is nearly finished.'

Ayamin touched my shirt, 'The only thing you need now is a haircut.'

The woman turned to Ayamin, 'And you my dear, we can't have you running around in rags with this handsome man beside you.'

Ayamin grinned, 'I wouldn't go as far as to say handsome....'

The two of them laughed again as they walked towards the women's section. I ran my hands over the new clothes feeling how soft and clean they were. The fabric felt light and when I looked in the mirror, I looked semi-decent, apart from the wad of dust-caked hair that sat on my head.

I heard Ayamin laugh again and felt something warm in my stomach. She hadn't laughed this much since we got to Budapest. She emerged from the changing rooms like a princess and spun around to show me the pastels of her outfit.

I clapped, 'Next stop Paris fashion week.'

Half an hour later Ayamin and I walked down the street arm in arm, feeling for all the world like a royal couple strolling around in our finery. Ayamin even tried her best high-class English accent. The woman had given us both jackets and even managed to slip in a pair of scissors for the haircuts.

We climbed up large white steps into a park and found ourselves a little secluded area among the shade of the trees. I sat and Ayamin bent down to kiss my forehead.

'Hair cut time.'

She pulled out the scissors, then knelt behind me with her legs touching my back. I closed my eyes as her hands slowly wove through my far too long hair. She gently snipped away at what I'd grown. The hair fell in small patches and I smiled as Ayamin touched both sides of my head. Completely focused on making it level. Her arm ran around my neck and I had this sudden urge to kiss her.

'Danny!! Do you realise how close you were to a bald spot just then?'

I moved my head back into place, 'It'd be worth it.'

'Come on Danny, I've got to get you looking semi-presentable.'

She gently trimmed my hair until she was happy with it. Meanwhile, little birds came around and picked up the pieces of hair that had drifted away from us.

'Insulation,' Ayamin said, tossing a clump of the hair to a robin, 'They know winter's going to be cold this year.'

After what seemed like hours of careful sculpting Ayamin sat back with a nod of contentment.

'I think that's as good as I'll get it.'

She passed me the scissors and took a seat in front of me. I stared at the scissors as she ran her hands through her hair, pulling out the knots, 'It's your turn to be the hairdresser.'

I tried to smile away the look of utter incompetence that crossed my face, but Ayamin caught it.

'Danny,' she said in a low voice, 'I don't care what you do to my hair, as long as it's not a mohawk or a mullet.'

I cocked my head, 'I think you'd look really hot in a mullet though.'

'Aww thanks. *But no.*'

I ran my hands through her hair, feeling the rough edges. Ayamin leant back against me. Slowly I began to snip away.

'I can't wait for England,' she said, 'I can't wait to stop being a refugee and just get on with the rest of my life.'

There were pieces of mud between a few strands. I combed my hand through, then cut. Her dark hair fell away from her head and gathered in little tufts on the ground.

'I want to become a nurse,' she said.

My hand slowed and she tilted her head back to look at me with those dark brown eyes of hers. I traced my thumb lightly over her forehead.

'I think that's amazing.'

Her grin was like the sun as she tilted her head back down.

'There aren't many jobs in this world where no matter what you're doing you're always trying to help someone.' As I bent in front of her to trim her fringe she looked into my eyes. 'I've missed a lot of schooling though.'

That made me laugh. I lowered the scissors and stared back.

'Look at you! If walking all of Turkey, Greece, Macedonia, Serbia, and avoiding drowning on the Aegean Sea couldn't stop you from getting here, I don't think a little missed schoolwork could stop you from anything.'

She tried to smile, but her eyes were watering. She leaned forward and the side of her nose brushed mine. Her lips were soft and tough, hot and cool. She moved forwards, kissed my cheek, then the tip of my ear.

'Oh Danny,' she whispered, 'I think this is the best haircut I've ever had.'

I started to chuckle. I couldn't help myself. Ayamin was giggling too. I wiped away the tears on her cheeks and then tried to suppress my laughter, but it bubbled back to the surface. Ayamin lost it and we ended up rolling around on the ground for about five minutes until the laughs had subsided. Then we hugged and I finished cutting her hair.

When half of it lay on the ground for the bird's nests, I took a step back and eyed it critically.

'Not bad,' I said... 'Not bad at all.'

Ayamin stood up. We walked to a small fountain and peered in the water. The change was drastic. I splashed some water on my face. I looked... *great.* She'd managed to trim the sides short and the bruises I'd got during the street fight had almost faded away. I looked like I could pass for a respectable young professional.

Ayamin elbowed me, 'You did good Danny,' she checked both sides of her hair, 'They're even the same length!'

I acted like it was nothing, 'I have been known to be a bit of an artist from time to time.'

She laughed and jumped on my back, both arms around my neck, 'Okay then Mr Con Artist, let's see how good you are at convincing these bank tellers.'

It was only as the two of us walked arm in arm to the CCD Bank that I began to have my doubts about the plan. I'd been missing from the Red Cross for over two months, *what if they've closed my account?*

We stepped through the door and she gave my hand a little squeeze.

'Good luck,' she whispered as she went to stand by the wall.

I joined the line and tried to casually glance up at the security cameras that peered down at me. I could feel my breathing increase. There were five foreigners lined up in front of me, and two bank tellers serving us.

I glanced backwards and was met with a stare from the burly security guard.

The two customers at the tellers moved away and the rest of us shuffled forward. A family came through the doorway and stood behind me. I tried to breathe slowly to keep calm.

It's not like I'm going to rob the bank, I told myself, *just chill out.* Yet even then I wasn't able to relax, at the bottom of my stomach I had a bad feeling about getting out the money, I just couldn't tell what it was.

The bank tellers moved quickly and I soon found myself standing at the front of the line. I glanced back at Ayamin and reminded myself why I was doing this.

'Hello sir?'

I looked across and saw a young bank teller calling me, I let out a sigh and walked over.

'You speak English?' I asked.

The woman nodded, 'Sure do sir, most of our customers do... now how can I help?'

'I need some cash,'

The woman nodded, 'Do you have your card?'

I shook my head, 'That's why I came to see you, my bag disappeared at the hostel I was at. Now I'm running low on money.'

The woman gave a sympathetic smile, 'Ah... a traveller's worst nightmare. You've contacted your embassy about it?'

I nodded, 'They're getting me a new passport.'

She smiled, 'Your name?'

'Danny Frey.'

'And your customer number'

'76764455.'

'Okay Danny, I'll just give the British embassy a quick call, it shouldn't take very long.'

I shifted my feet as she picked up the phone and began dialling. The line had grown behind me. I wondered how hard it would be to get past them. Then there was the security guard, he'd have a head start on me. I tried to control my breathing. I was trapped.

The woman rolled her eyes as she waited for someone to pick up. The phone kept ringing and a small candlewick of hope began to burn inside of me.

This was quickly extinguished when the woman started to speak.

'Hello there, Vanessa Harman here from the CCD Bank in Budapest. I have a Mr Danny Frey here, he said he's lost his passport and ID, can you confirm.... Our number to call back on is....'

I breathed a sigh of relief as she ended the call.

'They sounded busy, do you want to come in in an hour or so and we can sort it out then?'

'Yeah, I guess that'd be okay... I was hoping to buy something for lunch and give home a call, even if I can just withdraw maybe a hundred pounds in Hungarian now and then come back for the rest...' I crossed my fingers as she screwed up her face.

'Okay that sounds fair, I just need you to answer a few security questions before I give you the money....'

Ten minutes later and thirty-six thousand forints richer I stepped out of the doors with Ayamin.

We walked down the street quite casually, but as soon as we were out of sight of the bank Ayamin jumped on me and gave me a massive hug.

'I can't believe you got away with it,' she looked down at the pile of notes in my hand, 'I wish you'd seen it earlier; we're going to live like kings!'

I stuffed the notes into my pocket and hugged her, 'Vienna here we come!!'

The smile on her face was enough for me in that moment. She looked so beautiful and happy as she skipped along the concrete. I didn't have the heart to tell her about the embassy. I'd let the world know where we were, and although the bad feeling in my gut had grown, I knew it was worth it to have Ayamin smiling.

****

We had one last task in Budapest before we found a bus.

The old busker-man wasn't playing his guitar when we arrived at the alleyway. Instead, he sat just watching people pass by.

He looked at us and our new haircuts, and our flash second-hand clothes. He seemed to understand. A small dip of his head let us know that he'd accept no thanks. A hand trailing the cobblestones let us know that it was the way of people on the road.

Look out for each other his eyes said.

I smiled, we waved, and then the old busker was gone.

****

We found a cheap bus that was travelling through the night and climbed aboard. Both of us gazed around as we moved up the aisle, expecting someone to yell at us that we were refugees and that we had to get off.

But the bus was silent. Some people breathed deep as they prepared to sleep. Others were texting with a quick tap-tap on their screens.

We took our seats near the back and felt the driver crunch the bus into gear.

With a jerk and a slight rumble, we left Budapest behind. I watched the city lights twinkle until they disappeared behind a hill. Ayamin and I looked at each other, she smiled. It was a hopeful smile, but also a tired smile.

****

The doors to our bus opened in Vienna just as the morning sun began to show. Thirty of us stepped off and rubbed the sleep from our eyes. Ayamin and I hadn't got much. We'd spent most of the trip talking about the next leg of our journey which would take us through Italy and then France. After that we talked about England and school and Syria and then she tried to convince me that *Two Hearts in the French Night* was the best book ever by reading sentences from it.

Samantha sat on the steps of the church waiting. The lights of Briancon were dark to save electricity – she had only the moon to find Rudy.

'See?' She'd said, 'It's like poetry – but without fancy words.'

As the bus drove off I hoisted the pack onto my shoulders, it seemed lighter than when I'd started carrying it, but maybe I'd got used to its weight. Ayamin did star jumps to get blood back into her arms and legs.

'What do you want to do first?' I asked.

'I want to do breakfast,' she said, 'And a proper breakfast – not some half-eaten McDonalds.'

'How about that?' I asked, pointing in the direction of a shop that had a massive pancake sign sitting on top of it.

'Oh yeah!'

****

After exploiting the pancake house's 'all you can eat' policy we stumbled out of the shop clutching at our bellies.

I counted our money, we had about fifteen pounds left. *Not quite enough for another bus ride.*

We passed old castles, churches, and sleek modern mansions as we walked through Vienna. Stylish young people moved quickly through the city streets dressed in crisp yellows and blacks and whites and reds.

Ayamin sat on the bag while I held out my thumb at the edge of a busy south-bound motorway. We'd been waiting about half an hour when I spotted a sky-blue van with a field of flowers painted on it weaving through the traffic.

As the van got closer, I could hear hippy-music blasting from it, and then the scream of its engine.

The van pulled into the lane closest to us and skidded to a stop in front of me. The window opened. There was a young woman in the passenger's seat with an easy smile, next to her a wild-haired, bare-chested guy in his twenties yelled at us in what was probably Austrian.

I shook my head, 'English?'

His face brightened, 'Ah... English, very good, where are you critters headed?'

'England.'

'Ahh of course. We're going to Italy if you want a ride?'

I looked to Ayamin, she was loosening the straps on her backpack.

The side door of the van slid open, in the seat opposite us was a guy wearing a green shirt with a white clover on it. An unlit joint dangled in his mouth.

'They've got the road dust on them,' he said, then lit the joint.

I glanced at Ayamin and rolled my eyes slightly, *Are we sure we want to get into this van?*

She shrugged, *it's a ride I guess.*

We climbed in and went for the back seat. While the outside had been a tapestry of colours the inside seemed stripped bare of everything – including the seat headrests.

'If you'd caught me a week earlier,' the guy driving yelled, 'You'd have had the greatest seat in the history of seats, but we had to sell everything to pay for gas.'

We took off onto the road with a jerk. The driver picked up his phone and tapped at it. Music began pumping from a speaker at the front of the van.

'Whose van?' I yelled over the music.

The driver spun in his seat, clutching the wheel but not facing the road, 'It's mine. I'm Dean, from the Netherlands.' He pointed to the woman that sat in the front seat, 'That's Mila – I picked her up at a nightclub in France, and in the back with you is Conor from Ireland. He doesn't talk much. But when he does he says a lot.'

Conor nodded his head to the beat.

'And how about you?' Mila said, 'Where have you come from?'

'England,' I yelled, 'But we've just come from Hungary.'

'Ahh, I dig that,' Dean yelled, 'I'm trying to see as much of the world as possible, as fast as possible,' he turned his attention back to the road, narrowly avoiding a collision with a freight truck.

Dean drove like a madman for the next two hours, yelling his philosophies on life back to us as he went.

In the afternoon, when clouds started to appear on the horizon, he swerved into a gas station.

'Caca!' He yelled, 'Caca!!' Then wrenched on the handbrake and dived for the nearest petrol pump.

'What's Caca?' Ayamin said.

Mila was halfway through the passenger's door.

'It's French for poop, and I wish I never taught it to him,' she gestured to the gas station, 'Basically, we have until the car's finished filling to go to the bathroom, stretch our legs, and buy something. If we're not in the car by that point he swears he'll drive off without us.'

My eyes met Ayamin's, we both grinned and dove for the door.

Outside the van, I stretched my legs and walked into the petrol station. We couldn't afford to buy anything. But I liked looking. I imagined what I'd be able to buy when we got to England.

I knew that chips would be near the top of the list – good old impractical, hardly filling, chips. I could just about taste the crunch as I wandered the two aisles of the petrol station.

A television screen in the corner of the station caught my eye. Like the store itself, it was small, rectangular and low quality. But sitting there on the screen with tears dripping down her face, was Donna, the Red Cross woman.

I felt like I'd been slapped, and it only got worse when the television show host appeared on screen again, accompanied by two photos of me. There was a big red WANTED written at the bottom of the screen. The host was interviewing a police officer.

Why do they care? I wondered as my mouth hung open, *there are millions of people in Europe. Why do I make the news?*

They switched back to Donna. She was crying. The title they'd given her was 'Former Red Cross Team Leader.'

Former.

I glanced at the cashier, he was busy helping Dean, Mila was flicking through a magazine rack, Conor was outside smoking something illegal, and Ayamin: she was... in the toilet.

I breathed out. Glanced up at the T.V screen. They'd put up a security camera picture of me in the bank. I crossed my fingers. Mila had given up on the magazines... she was turning around. She saw the T.V, and let out a gasp.

'Dean, look at that!'

Dean and the cashier turned. I think Dean swore.

'Really? *Really?* How the hell did we lose to France again?'

I turned to the screen. The news programme had switched to sport. The Netherlands had taken a thumping in the football.

While Mila taunted him I let out a laugh of relief, 'That was damn close.'

Dean shook his head, 'It wasn't close. We don't know what we're doing on the field this year.'

Back on the road, everyone else took turns roasting the Netherlands football team. Dean, their most loyal supporter was also their harshest critic.

'Conor. You, me and Mila could give them a whipping. We'll make our own team. This can be our tour bus.'

Conor shook his head, 'I've got the reflexes of a whale.'

'You'll still be better than The Flying Dutchmen,' Ayamin yelled.

There was a chorus of cheers from Mila and Conor, and sobbing from Dean.

But all the fun seemed muted to me. My mind just kept cycling back to the gas station. It seemed like the world was closing in on me.

And I haven't even told Ayamin yet.

That was the part that was freaking me out. *How's she going to react? How am I going to tell her?* I could feel my past catching up with me.

'Danny?'

I looked away from the window. Ayamin was staring at me. She had a smile on her face.

'All good Danny?'

I shrugged, trying to put myself back in the moment, 'Yeah I'm good.'

I slapped a fake smile on my face and raised my voice, 'Better than the Netherlands national football team anyway.'

Everyone laughed. But Ayamin didn't laugh quite as much as the others. She nudged my shoulder with her chin, 'Are you sure?'

'I'm sure Aya.'

Ayamin nodded and leaned her head against my shoulder, 'It's getting dark outside.'

Out the window, the first stars were beginning to appear. They flickered and disappeared when we passed through towns, but re-joined our journey in the countryside. I looked at Ayamin, she had this warm sleepy smile on her face that broke my heart a little.

Forget about it, I told myself, *enjoy this Danny, live in the moment.*

I wrapped my arm around her and tried to focus on the rise and fall of her body as she breathed. Her eyes closed and not long after she slumped against me.

'People's faces never lie when they're asleep,' Connor said from the seat in front of me, 'You've got a genuine human right there Danny.'

I stared at him, and his hoody pulled up around his head.

'I know. Hell, I know.'

He smiled and nodded away to some beat in his head. I turned back to the window and wondered, *what does my face look like when I'm asleep?*

****

I was hot, had a sore neck, and felt kind of sick when the sun woke me. Armed with a twelve-pack of Pepsi Dean hadn't stopped all night. The twisting and turning of the van meant sleep was snatched five minutes at a time.

When I blinked my eyes open, I saw the front seats and then the back seats were empty. I stood, feeling like I was about to throw up, and opened the passenger's door.

The first thing that made me smile was the scent – almost minty but more comforting. Then there was the colour – light purple stretching as far as the eye could see. We were in the lavender fields.

'Danny!' Ayamin said, lavender hung from the French braid in her hair, 'You slept in.'

I stepped out of the van. It was almost like stepping into a fairy tale – only Dean was swearing loudly in Dutch from the other side of the van.

'What's going on?'

Ayamin took a lavender stem and put it behind my ear. She smiled, 'Apparently we got a flat tyre in the middle of the night. Dean got like two hours of sleep and spent the rest of the time yelling at the wheel for getting a puncture.'

We walked around the van to where the wheel was propped off the ground on a flimsy tyre jack.

Mila sat on her bag watching Dean kick the deflated tyre across the road. He yelled in Dutch for half a minute before flopping into a sitting position on the road.

'That's the last time I try to take a shortcut.'

Mila laughed, 'You said the same thing in Germany and Austria!'

Dean joined her laughter, 'Yeah I suppose I did.'

'Do you have a spare?' I asked.

'Nah I had to sell it for gas, along with pretty much every other tool that would be useful right now.'

He sighed and looked around, 'Damn these are cool fields. I really dig the colour purple, and the scent, and Mila you look gorgeous this morning.'

He got up, threw the tyre back onto our side of the road and picked up Mila bridal style.

'I'm going to make the most of this,' he said, kissing her mouth and grinning and running for the lavender fields all in the same moment. Mila was screaming with laughter.

Ayamin stood opened mouth as they disappeared behind a row of lavender.

'Are all Europeans this crazy?'

I shrugged, 'Only when it comes to football.'

My fingers slid into her hand, 'Where's Conor gone?'

She moved closer, her legs brushed mine, and her free hand moved up my shoulder, 'He said he was going to find something to smoke. He's been gone a while.'

'Well, we're alone,' I said.

'I think you're right,' she said.

My lips found hers, her mouth was hot and her hands found my chest. The smooth skin of her waist felt heavenly under my rough finger...

'Hey guys.'

We froze. I turned my head to see Conor standing on the road with sunglasses on, a smoking blunt in his mouth, and a wheel under his bare foot.

Conor shrugged, 'I found a new tyre.'

Ayamin touched my ear, 'Let's finish this later,' she whispered. Reluctantly I let her go.

Conor seemed oblivious to everything. He had a serene smile on his face.

'Seriously Conor where'd you get the tyre?' I asked.

He pointed down the road, 'I was just walking along looking at the flowers and then bam! There's a wheel in my hand and I thought to myself, that's serendipity because we were just looking for a tyre.'

Aya shook her head, 'Serendipity?'

Conor stared out into the field. That serene smile floated over his lips again.

'It's kind of like when two stones from different beaches fit perfectly into each other.'

He took a long drag on his joint and exhaled. The scent of it mixed with the lavender. We waited for Conor to speak again, but he seemed content with just standing there smoking.

Ayamin helped me roll Conor's wheel over to the van and with dusty fingers, we put the wheel back on.

Dean and Mila arrived back at the van just after we'd finished and Ayamin told Mila about the wheel appearing in Conor's hands.

Mila just rolled her eyes.

'That's the sort of thing he's always doing.'

She walked over to Conor, took his sunglasses off, and gazed into his eyes.

'Did he mention serendipity?'

One laugh was all the confirmation she needed.

'Dean, Conor's wasted.'

Dean just shrugged as he finished his inspection of the 'new' wheel.

'Who cares? The road's waiting baby.'

With an insane grin on his face, Dean ran over to Conor and wrapped an arm around him.

'Let's go! Go! Go! Go!'

We ran for the van and barely had time to get in our seats before Dean threw the van into gear, sending dust flying.

The van thundered down the narrow country road. We screamed around a corner and swerved past a police van sitting on the side of the road.

'Damn,' Dean said as the police van's lights flashed and it pulled out onto the road, 'There's no way we can outrun them.'

But the police van had other ideas. It skidded back onto the grass edge of the road, then refused to budge.

'Oh my,' Mila said as we zoomed off, 'They've only got three wheels.'

Ayamin and I exchanged a look, then stared at Conor who was flopped backwards in his seat. He breathed out a puff of smoke, then spoke one word:

'Serendipity.'

****

It was all going so well until Dean's Bluetooth speaker gave out.

He'd had it pumping the entire ride, and danced to everything from reggae tunes to house music. Without the speaker, the van suddenly seemed much quieter.

The sun had almost set again and there were black rings around Dean's eyes. In the distance, we could see the lights of Milan.

Ayamin and Mila were talking, Connor was sleeping and Dean was fidgeting with the wheel.

'Are you sure it won't go?' he asked Mila.

'It's not going to go, Dean, just like the twenty other times you asked.'

He swore and tapped on the steering wheel. Then turned his attention to the radio.

'I'm getting a little desperate.'

He flicked it on, an Italian pop song was playing.

The voice was soft and sweet and it was the sort of tune you could bop your head to.

'What's she saying?' Dean asked Mila.

'She's talking about a girl – but she's not just a girl she's also the sun.'

Dean reached over and rubbed Mila's shoulder, 'Could you?...'

She rolled her eyes, 'You always ask me to...'

'I know. But you're so good at it.'

'Fine,' Mila said, she turned down the volume of the radio slightly and began to translate the words.

'Then one day she floated free.
She was too much, and not enough for he.

She had no more space,
And took to the stars.

Running her own race,
And bringing light to ours.

But when she saw her light reflected,
The feeling was more than she'd expected.'

We sat in silence after the song ended. Mila's voice had a hypnotic tone.

Then a beeping came over the radio and a news broadcaster started delivering quick bursts of information in Italian.

Dean looked at Mila, and with a roll of her eyes, she continued translating.

'blah blah blah... something about a new tax hurting people in Milan... um... The hunt for a British teenager who went missing from an aid programme in Turkey has resumed after the teenager was spotted in a bank in Austria.'

I drew in a breath and glanced sideways. Ayamin was looking at me, but everyone else seemed oblivious.

'Danny Frey, now eighteen, was sent on the Red Cross expedition after he was convicted of the robbery and vandalism of a liquor store.'

As the announcer went further into my background, I felt Ayamin lean away from me. Her face had gone pale and her eyes burned into mine until I had to look away.

Dean had stopped tapping on the steering wheel and when he looked into the rear-view mirror, I knew that he knew.

When Mila was midway through translating a sentence, Dean reached across and turned the radio off.

Apart from the van's whine, we sat in silence. Milan's street signs flew past. I looked at Ayamin, she stared straight at me, straight into my eyes and soul. A tear flowed freely down her nose.

Conor woke up. Stretched out his legs. My throat was almost too dry to breathe.

'I'll drop you here,' Dean said, pulling off the motorway.

Ayamin hoisted up our bag, and I slumped my way out the door after her.

'Thanks for the ride Dean,' I said.

He nodded, 'Take care.'

The colourful van pulled away into the traffic. Its engine strained as it tried to accelerate.

Ayamin stood on the footpath, she was just over a meter away from me, but it felt like all the distance in the world. Her eyes gazed straight into mine and I had to look away. *You have messed up Danny-boy,* I thought to myself, *you've darn messed up.*

'Sh-should we find somewhere to sit and talk about this?' I asked, feeling like I was talking to a stranger.

Ayamin didn't say a thing. Her eyes remained on my face, but she did nod at least.

Sheltered from the road by a stand of trees stood a white concrete wall. I climbed on top of it and looked out over Milan. An orange sun was setting on the horizon and bathed the city in its glow.

Ayamin fumbled her way to the top of the wall.

She sat there, staring at me. Her cheek had small lines of orange on it from where her tears reflected the sunset. I reached out to wipe at it, but Ayamin jerked backwards without a word.

I pulled my hand back and stared out at the sun again.

'The reason I lied to you about the refugee camp is I was scared you wouldn't want to have anything to do with me. I wanted you to see me as more than a criminal.'

I waited for her to say something... her eyes were intense, almost magnetised to mine and her mouth hung open slightly, but she didn't speak so I continued.

'After that, I just couldn't find the right time – or the bravery to tell you... and it's more than that; I started to feel like a different person – a good person. Because of you, I wanted to be someone better – and that's who I became. Meeting you was like a fresh start Ayamin. I didn't want that tarnished with the bad things I'd done before.'

I paused and breathed in. My heart was beating way too fast. I felt almost angry – but not quite. Ayamin just sat there. Watching.

'Umm,' I said, 'That's it... you're the best thing that's ever happened to me Ayamin and I love you and I hope you can see that the only reason I didn't tell you before is because I was scared to lose you.'

She sat. waiting for me to speak again. I let the silence hang. I wanted to hear from her – I desperately wanted to hear her say *something.*

Ayamin let out a sigh and jumped down from the wall, swung the bag onto her back, and walked off. Her boots tapped on the concrete path and every step seemed to echo.

I got to my feet. I was ready to chase her, to beg her like I had when we left the refugee camp, but then I stopped.

She's just found out that the guy she's been travelling with is a wanted criminal. She needs space.

I sat back down on the wall. It felt colder now that the sun had set.

It got colder and colder as I waited for Ayamin to come back. Below me I watched clubs begin to open up and foreigners walk out of supermarkets carrying bags bulging with alcohol.

I shivered, stood up and looked around. No Ayamin. I kicked at the wall, imagining it was my face, then toppled off and grazed my forehead on the ground.

'Woah buddy, you alright?'

I moaned as a group of university students gathered around me.

'He's cracked his head,' one of the girls said, she had an English accent.

'Nah,' I said, sitting up, 'I've just cracked my heart.'

The group gave a sympathy 'Ahhh,' and two of the guys helped me to my feet. They placed a half-empty bottle of wine in my hands then wandered off.

I went back to the wall and leaned against it. I took a swig of the wine. It tasted terrible.

A girl called out, I turned, but it was just some backpacker calling out to their friends. I took another drink. It still tasted like ass.

I let my feet fall from under me and sat on my butt clutching the wine bottle. *Surely she'll be here soon?* I took a good long swallow and decided I'd never drink cheap wine again.

There was a street party just down the road from where I was sitting. People were laughing as they stumbled out of it with their arms around each other. That's all I wanted, just to go to the street party with Ayamin, we'd dance and we'd sing and we'd forget everything bad had happened. I took another swallow and decided to go check it out.

As I wobbled to my feet, I looked around for Ayamin. Nothing. She was gone. I drank. Tossed the empty bottle in the bin. I needed more alcohol.

The street party was a mass of colourful cloth, flags, and confetti. There were hundreds of people with painted faces singing along to Italian tunes.

I slipped in, wandering through the throngs of people and drinking discarded liqueurs and wines sitting on tables.

The music was bright party music. People bounced and twirled and smiled. Drinks spilled into my mouth and I felt a numb smile begin.

The beat changed but I was still swaying. I put my hand to my head just before I hit the ground. I felt my nose explode... little drips of blood floated past like flowers in the wind. I felt hands on my face. Soft hands and caring eyes.

'Ayamin?' I asked, 'Where did you go?'

****

I woke up on carpet so soft that for a moment I thought I was still dreaming. The carpet was white, the ceiling was white, the blanket stretched over me was white, but my head felt grey like a storm.

I stretched my arms. The room smelt good, like rose or strawberries.

'Morning.'

I sat up quickly, someone sat in the bed next to me, and that someone wasn't Ayamin.

Long, brown flecked hair. A foreign face. Where was she from? Britain? Scandinavia? Germany?

You're an idiot I told myself.

'Rough night?' she said in an accent that screamed Northern England.

I peered down at myself. I was naked from the waist up but thank goodness I still had chinos on. Still, I almost slapped myself in the face. *How am I going to explain this to Ayamin?*

'Good morning,' I said, watching her watching me. There was this awkward silence, I didn't know what to say to her and she didn't seem to know what to say to me. I wanted to ask about the night before but I was a little afraid.

'Who's Ayamin?' she asked.

I opened my mouth but didn't speak. I wanted to say that she was my girlfriend, travel buddy, partner. But I didn't know if that was true anymore.

The British girl hugged her pillow, 'Just the way you said her name... seems like you care about her a lot.'

I nodded, 'Ummm... Did we *do* anything last night?'

The girl laughed, it was a nice laugh, full of colour, 'No, you wouldn't even let me kiss you. When I tried you were all... Ayamin this... Ayamin that.'

I let out a breath, at least I hadn't made it worse for myself.

She looked a little sad, 'Why did you break up? I'd love someone as fit, tanned, and wholesome as you.'

'I'm not so sure wholesome should be on that list,' I shrugged, 'I've been lying to her since we met.'

'Oh... what about?'

This British girl seemed nice and all, but I found myself wondering, *What am I doing here? Why am I talking to her?*

I shrugged, looked up at the clock that sat on her wall, 'I should get going.'

'Are you sure? Do you want to grab some breakfast first?'

Despite the groan of my stomach, I shook my head, 'I've got somewhere to be.'

****

In daylight, the wall where Ayamin had left me looked like a grave. A solid concrete marker of what had been lost.

I sat cross-legged underneath the wall and watched people glide past. The stone I sat on was cold, and I shivered with hunger. I watched throngs of tourists move through the area. Shopkeepers yawned.

I waited until well past midday for Ayamin to show up before I walked past a McDonald's and swiped some leftovers people had left on their trays.

For water, I stopped by a group of ancient stone lions that had springs trickling from their mouths.

The water was supposed to be lucky, but even though I waited at the wall all afternoon there was no sign of my favourite traveller.

As dark approached, a conversed pair of feet appeared in front of me.

'Did she come?'

I looked up. It was the British girl. She seemed to already know my answer so I kept my mouth shut and looked back down at the concrete.

'You can't stay here all night.'

'I've done it before.'

She seemed at a loss for words. I was hungry and angry. I didn't want her pity.

With great care, the girl sat down on the concrete opposite me.

'Well, I guess I'm staying too.'

'Don't be stupid.'

'Look, either you're coming back to my place where it's warm and we can order Italian takeaway, or we're both going to sit here in the cold and die.'

I gave her my meanest stare, pushing all the hate and sadness and heartbreak I had in me towards her. The girl flinched but she stayed sitting.

My tummy rumbled and then I sighed, 'Okay you win.'

I stood, held out my hand, 'I'm Danny.'

She took it and gave a slight smile, 'Gianina.'

By the next morning, I was sitting on the wall before the sun had risen. Gianina joined me and we sat gazing out at the town. From our vantage point, she pointed to her favourite spaces. When we were hungry we ate, and when it got dark we went back to Gianina's house.

That night it began to rain, and as we ate breakfast the next morning Gianina glanced out the window and told me she had a busy day of catching up on Netflix ahead of her. I said I'd bring Ayamin back and we could all watch together. Gianina laughed, but her eyes seemed worried.

I sat in the rain in Gianina's pink jacket. The rain quickly soaked through my pants. The tip of my nose was impossibly cold.

People dashed in and out of buildings. The only colour was flashes of warm yellow light from the stores, everything else was a different shade of grey.

It grew dark and I kept sitting there – only I wasn't waiting – I was stuck. Ayamin and her quest had been my purpose, *my life,* for months. Suddenly I had nothing.

My teeth chattered between each breath. I tried to bury my hands under the coat to keep them warm, but that skin was just as cold.

'Danny! Danny!'

A tiny phone light appeared in the rain. Footsteps splashed in the puddle I was sitting in.

Gianina was yelling at me but her voice seemed muted and cold... We stumbled back to her flat and she pushed me, fully clothed, into the shower... She was hugging me and crying and the hot water was soaking through her clothes... Gianina pulled my jacket off and then my shirt... and then the two of us were sitting on the floor of her shower with hot water gushing over us...and then as the water thawed me I started to cry and talk. I told her about the journey. About Greece, Macedonia, riding trains, kissing under the stars, and cuddling in the cold.

'And now... and now it's all gone.'

Gianina had her arms around me, her skin was warmer than mine, she was crying too.

'Maybe that's okay Danny. Those memories make you sad now, but one day they'll make you smile.'

'She was everything. She made me a good person – and now what am I? I'm nothing. I'm a criminal.'

Gianina was kissing my bare shoulder, she was rubbing my back.

'I came here for an Italian boy. I gave up my job, said good-bye to my family, got a lease on this apartment and he dumped me after just a month. Everyone has breakups, Danny.'

'But I just thought we were more... we'd been through so much shit together... I thought we couldn't be separated.'

She shook her wet hair, 'I wouldn't have left you Danny. Seriously. I've never met anyone like you.' Gianina was looking into my eyes, and I saw in her face that same desperation I felt inside.

I looked away from her. The shower was starting to run cold. I turned it off, stood, and grabbed two towels.

'It's getting late.'

****

I woke before Gianina, and I was glad of that. The city streets were quiet as I walked them in the dawn light.

There's no way Ayamin's coming to find me, I thought as I passed the wall where she'd left me.

Not far from the wall was a bus stop, and next to it – a radio station. I walked past the bus stop and thought about travel, *she could already be in France – or even England.*

Something made me stop outside the radio station. It had its signs written in English and Italian. It made me wonder if perhaps there was a slight hope... *So I can't text or call her... but maybe there's another way?* A plan was beginning to form.

I fixed the address of the station in my head and hurried back to Gianina's. She was sitting in bed, and laughed when she saw me, 'Danny, it's good to see you smiling.'

'That's because I have a plan – I think I know how to get a message to Ayamin.'

Her face dropped, 'Oh... that's great.'

'I'm going to ask the radio station to put a message on, but it's got to be something only she will understand.'

I sat down on one of Gianina's chairs and glanced at her bookshelf – there on the upper left corner was a very familiar sight. *Two Hearts in the French Night.*

*****

I rubbed my eyes and tried to focus on the world around me, the Italian people, the shops, the smells.

Many blocks later I found myself standing outside the English radio house.

'She's worth it,' I reminded myself, 'She's worth it even if you can't convince her.'

Taking a breath, I walked into the radio house.

Inside I found that the radio house also shared its building with an accounting firm and a laundromat.

I walked into the radio place and rang the bell for reception, then sat on their lone chair. The only thing hanging from the walls was a menu for a local pizza place that looked about five years out of date.

After waiting a few minutes, a young woman's head popped through the reception window, 'Oh hello there!'

'Hello, I'm…' my nervous pitch was cut short as she disappeared. The sound of a bolt dropping came from a door to the reception.

'Ciao!' she said, shaking my hand, 'Come in I'll show you around.'

'Okay,' I said, my voice lifted a little in surprise.

The woman took me through the door and into the second half of their building which was marginally bigger than the reception area – only this one had two booths with microphones and sound pads and cables running everywhere.

'So that's Chris,' she said pointing at the man sitting in one of the sound booths, 'He's our journalist here, he prepares the news bulletins and sometimes does work for the BBC.' She waved her hand, 'Well very occasionally.'

'Then there's Andrea who's not here but sells our advertising.' She pointed to a desk between the booths, 'That's where Andrea works.'

She pointed to herself, 'I'm Caitlynn, and you're… *Brian*, right?'

'Ahh, Danny actually.'

She frowned for a moment, 'Sorry…. I swear I was told it was Brian… anyway let me introduce you to the equipment.'

Caitlynn took me through to the empty booth and sat me down in a chair in front of one of the microphones.

'Do international stations ever pick this up?'

Caitlynn shrugged, 'They're allowed to pick up pretty much whatever they want but basically don't. I think the last time someone picked up my station was two years ago when we had a big fire here and I spoke to the mayor. It does happen but only if it's big news or something crazy.'

I nodded, feeling rather sure my story would qualify as at least crazy.

She checked her watch, 'Hey sorry to throw this at you on your first day, but I'm going live in like thirty seconds, want to join me?'

I grinned, 'Yeah that's what I was hoping for... but what do you mean by first day?'

She smiled, adjusting knobs and switches, 'Well I hope you're going to come back. It gets boring here by myself.'

I went to speak, to try to explain that we were both talking about two completely different things but Caitlynn held her hand up, 'And we're live in *5 - 4 - 3...*'

I drew in a breath and ran a palm over my forehead. *This is not what I was expecting.*

'Hello and welcome to Radio Milan, your favourite English language show, the time is currently nine o'clock and we're here for the first time with my new co-host Danny!'

I sat unsure how to respond, Caitlynn stared at me for just a few seconds before leaning over her microphone again, 'Why don't you tell us a bit about yourself.'

I nodded and looked from her to my microphone, 'Actually I'm not trying to become a co-host.'

Caitlynn's eyes went wide, 'That's why I thought your name was Brian,' she gave a nervous laugh, 'He must've never shown up.'

I nodded, wringing my hands a little as she thought for just a split second,

'Well, on radio we have two golden rules – one is that you must never say these words,' she held up a sheet with a list of swear words on it, 'And the other is to never have 'dead air' – to never let the radio go silent. That's basically all you need to know to have a career in radio Danny.'

She grinned, but it was still slightly forced, 'Why don't you tell us why you came to our station in the first place, we don't usually get social calls.'

I grinned, 'We have an hour, right?'

Caitlynn shrugged, 'More or less.'

I nodded and began to tell my story.

'It was Friday, a school day, and once again I was stuck in court…'

I told Caitlynn everything, or as near to everything I could fit into one hour. At the start she interrupted a few times, 'How old were you? What about your parents? Why did you follow her?'

But as the journey wore on, she fell silent, and for a long time, I felt like I couldn't see her anymore. Instead, my eyes were focused on the inflatable we'd used to travel to Greece, the waiting in the North Macedonia camp, the old man with the weed and the guitar in Budapest, by the time I arrived back here at the radio house we'd gone ten minutes overtime and Caitlynn had been silent for over half an hour.

'And the last thing I want to say is Ayamin I am so sorry for lying to you. I'm an idiot, but I'm also an idiot that can't go without you. In a week I'm going to be in the same place that Samantha sat waiting – the place where the lights were dark to save electricity – and where she only had the moon to find Rudy.

Please come and see me. *Please.* I'm an idiot, but even idiots deserve second chances.'

I sniffed, wiped my nose then looked at Caitlynn, 'I think that's all I wanted to say.'

Caitlynn's eyes looked as far away as mine had been, they refocused and then she broke the first golden rule of radio by swearing her head off, 'I think I believe you.'

I nodded, and for the next five minutes she broke the second golden rule – she fell silent and just stared ahead like she was trying to process what happened. Eventually, she seemed to come to her senses and flicked a few knobs.

Bon Jovi's *Living on a Prayer* came on – sort of a fitting theme song, I guess. The door next to us burst open and Chris the journalist came in.

'The BBC want it.'

They want what?' I asked, as Caitlynn continued to stare ahead.

'They want your interview,' said Chris, 'Is it true?'

I nodded.

Chris shook his head and now he was staring too, Damn man, damn.'

'Y-you said the government was after you?' Caitlynn said.

'Of course, they are,' said Chris, 'His face has been plastered across the news for the last few days.'

'Then you've got to get out of here,' said Caitlynn, 'They're probably on their way.'

I nodded and stood to my feet just as Chris's phone rang.

'Hold up,' he said as I moved past him to the door, 'It's the BBC,' he called.

Caitlynn unlocked the door and pushed me through reception and onto the street.

'CNN, the Guardian, they all want you, Danny,' Chris yelled behind me.

I started to run and for a minute it looked like Chris would try to follow me to Gianina's. But I'd walked thousands of kilometres to get here, I was lean and fit. Chris, who worked a desk job, didn't stand a chance.

By the time I reached Gianina's, there were two helicopters in the air. In the distance, I heard sirens wailing and I gulped as I pushed through the door.

'I did it,' I called.

Gianina emerged from the kitchen and threw a hug around me.

'You were gone for ages,' she said, 'Did you manage to get anyone international?'

I grinned, 'All of them by the sounds of it.'

Her eyes lit up and she ran to the edge of the kitchen, grabbing a full backpack.

'Follow me,' she said, rushing out the door.

I nearly crashed into her as I leapt outside.

Gianina was staring up at the sky, her mouth hanging open the way Caitlynn's had.

'Is that two Italian police helicopters I see,' she asked.

I peered past her, then shrugged, 'I can't read Italian.'

Gianina shook her head, a mad grin settling on her face, 'I think you may have outdone yourself Danny.'

We raced down to the small garage that sat beneath her flat. A Vespa scooter sat next to a pile of canvas. Gianina took a hold of the canvas and in one swift motion lifted it from the heap.

'Ta-da!' she said, revealing a second Vespa scooter – this one light blue.

'Wow,' I said, running a finger over it. Scratches ran along its sides and a faint hint of rust was showing on the handlebars, but overall it was a thing of beauty.

'I hope you're not giving this to me.'

Gianina laughed, 'Of course I am, you need it to complete your quest.'

Her craziness made me grin, 'I couldn't take this from you Gianina.'

She made the sound horses do when they don't like something, 'You'd actually be helping me out, this is my ex-boyfriend's scooter – the same one who ditched me.'

'Really?'

'I haven't seen him for two months and as far as I'm concerned a burglar came one night and stole it.'

I smiled as I sat on the seat, felt the accelerator.

'I used to call him Henry,' said Gianina, running a hand through her hair.

'Who?'

'The Vespa, I don't know if you want to change it or anything but the Vespa always seemed like a Henry to me.'

'Henry the Vespa,' I said, 'Perfect.'

I kick-started Henry and watched the fuel level rise to only a fraction above empty.

'Here's the helmet,' said Gianina, passing me a fluro-pink item.

'What's this?' I asked.

'Your helmet,' she said, 'I'm sorry, my ex broke the other one.'

I shoved on the helmet and Gianina passed me the bag she'd been carrying. It was heavy and full – two qualities I'd learnt to appreciate in my time as a refugee.

'Food – clothes – love,' she said, kissing my helmet. 'Now go! Go find your Ayamin.'

'Thank you Gianina – for everything,' I started to say, 'I'm going to owe you for th-'

'You don't have time to owe me. There are police helicopters in the sky – GO!'

I pushed the throttle as far as I could and felt Henry wheelie as I made it out onto the street.

****

Milan wasn't quite as easy to escape as I'd anticipated. I got lost three times before I found the main highway out.

Being chased by police didn't help – every time I heard a siren, I'd turn into a sideroad or alleyway and wait to see if anything would pass. When they didn't Henry and I would slip back around the corner while I tried to work out which way I'd been going.

Eventually, I found myself on the highway. A large sign indicated that France was only 240 kilometres away and I threw back the throttle so far that little Henry began to whine. Still, it wasn't quite enough to keep up with the cars that flashed past us. I kept well to the right, but even then, the rush of wind and occasional spraying of gravel were my constant companions.

I'd been on the highway for half an hour when two things happened at once. Firstly, I noticed a blue and red flicker in Henry's sole wing mirror. Turning my head and wobbling, I saw a police car weaving its way through the traffic in my direction, I revved Henry a little harder.

The second thing I noticed was his fuel gauge sitting on empty which put to bed any ideas of trying to outrun the cops.

I'd spotted what looked like a petrol station around a kilometre back and considered pulling a U-turn. However, four lanes of speeding cars to my left made me rethink this idea.

I peered back; the lights were getting closer. My orange fuel light had come on. *Time to make a decision Danny.*

So, I did, there was a ditch next to me. Nothing too deep, but enough to cover me and a scooter named Henry.

I slowed slightly, watching my wing mirror until the police car's view was blocked by a large truck, then I swerved into the ditch.

Poor Henry's suspension made a cracking sound as we left the road and his engine died as we landed in the ditch. I didn't fare much better. The ground slipped from beneath us and my arm got crushed underneath Henry.

While I rubbed my elbow the two of us crouched in the drain, waiting with bated breath for the police car. Five minutes passed, then ten. I unscrewed Henry's wing mirror and held it up, using it like a periscope to check the road. No police cars were in sight.

I pulled Henry's keys from his ignition and placed my distinctive pink helmet to one side. Moving in a crouch, I made my way back along the drain towards the petrol station. When I got there the pump attendant was watching a television screen. On it, police helicopters were flying over the city.

I bought a small jerry can and filled it with petrol. The attendant hardly looked at me when I paid for the fuel, as I placed the money on the bench between us the man said something in Italian and pointed at the screen.

Then he frowned and an odd expression came onto his face. He turned back to me.

I grabbed my fuel and left. Walking towards the drain as fast as I could without actually running. The man came out of the store and shouted something at me in Italian. I didn't turn around.

The moment I got within sight of the drain I was sprinting. By the time I reached Henry, my throat felt raw.

I grabbed the key, unscrewed his tank and poured the fuel into it, spilling a little as I went.

With the tank full, I used a piece of rubber to tie the spare fuel onto Henry's seat, then hauled him up onto the road again.

Panting, I kick-started his motor and the sweet little scooter roared to life immediately. I threw on my fluro helmet and sped away.

****

That repeating pattern became my life for the next sixteen hours, every time I spotted a cop trailing me, I'd throw myself and Henry off the road. Twice I had to stop near petrol stations to get refills and both times I thought about sleeping. But I knew that I had to get as much distance between me and the city as possible.

Plus, every kilometre that ticked over on the scooter's speedometer felt like one kilometre closer to Ayamin. It was only as I was approaching the afternoon of my second day that I had to stop. I found myself wobbling into the lanes next to me and was woken from my half-sleep by the horn of a truck, I only just swerved myself and Henry out of its way before it squashed us.

Henry and I crawled under the shelter of a lone tree in some farmer's paddock off to the side of the highway. While Henry rested his engine, I dug into the bag Gianina had given me and pulled out a ton of Italian food.

After demolishing eight slices of an enormous pizza and washing it down with water from a nearby creek, I crawled under a woollen blanket and tried to fall asleep. Roots beneath my back meant I kept shifting around, trying to find a more comfortable position.

I thought about Ayamin, I wondered where she would be right now, and if she'd got my message.

The moon arrived. I thought about how strange it was that Aya and I could be lying on the same stretch of road, potentially just a few kilometres away from each other and looking at the same moon.

At some point, I fell asleep.

****

The next day it began to rain. I thought about staying under my tree and crashing there for the day but the thought of missing my meeting with Ayamin kept me going.

'Come on Henry,' I said, loading him up with my belongings, 'Time to go buddy.'

Towns and trees and turnoffs passed and eventually Henry the Vespa crawled up the slope towards Briancon – the same place I'd read about with Ayamin.

I could've pushed him harder, could've revved his little engine like crazy, but Henry had got me this far, that pastel blue workhorse had managed to carry me all the way to France.

Plus, I reckoned we still had a few kilometres to go after we got to Briancon, hopefully with one more passenger.

There was one other reason I was driving like a snail. It was the main reason. The one deep inside of me that I didn't want to think about.

I was going slow because I worried that Ayamin might not be there. It was like the longer I took to get to Briancon the longer I still had a chance of her being there.

At the same time, all I wanted was to get to the top and see her. So, I was in this strange crazy conundrum – some might call it love.

I laughed out loud and listened to it ricochet from the walls that made up the edge of town.

A few people were wandering the streets of Briancon, some were tourists buying handcrafted jerseys. They watched me as I rode the Vespa as slowly as I could through town.

It doesn't matter, I thought, *because she said she loved you too. She's probably thinking the same thing that you are. She's probably up there pacing away and wondering where that idiot got to.*

I increased the speed of Henry as a smile rode on my face, *she's waiting for you,* I told myself as the church steeples appeared. There was something about the church, it almost made me want to get married.

My thought train stopped as Henry rounded the sloped street, the whole church was standing before me. The lights had just come on and even in the evening light they illuminated the steps, and sitting on the steps waiting patiently was...

No one.

****

Hope is a very dangerous thing.

Hope meant I sat on the steps of that church until both the moon and stars had come out. I sat there shivering until

I was forced to admit that she probably wasn't going to show up tonight. When nearly everyone had gone to bed, I parked Henry a little way behind the church and found a gutter to climb up.

After dislodging a little snow from the roof, I climbed into a sort of cave made by one of the building's spires and spread out my lone blanket.

Things were a little colder in the mountains, but I still managed some sleep.

In the morning I ate, climbed down and sat at the steps waiting. *Today's the day,* I told myself. As I waited a few locals came and talked to me. They asked their questions in French which didn't make things easy for either party. The two languages I spoke – Arabic and English were probably the two least useful languages to speak in that part of France. The moment I said a word of either most people just turned their heads and walked away.

Not that it particularly bothered me. I had more important things on my mind. Top of the list was – *where is Ayamin?*

I waited, and waited, and waited some more. The whole day I sat on that church step, watching the world go by, and of course, waiting. I wasn't patient. Every time someone emerged on the other side of the town square I leapt to my feet. Every time was a disappointment.

I felt like kicking the church down.

The day wore on. Members of the church gathered inside. After they'd finished singing French hymns an old gentleman with an English accent offered me some bread. I took it and thanked him as he disappeared inside.

The sun went down and so did my hopes of seeing Ayamin again. She wasn't there.

Like a sloth, I climbed back up onto the roof of the church where I pulled my blanket over me, but that night I couldn't sleep.

The sun rose and I shivered in my blanket, but when I touched my skin it felt hot.

I crawled from the roof of the church; my muscles barely functioning as I climbed my way down the guttering. I fell the last two meters.

When I reached the church steps, I pushed olives from the jar Gianina had given me into my mouth and hoped their saltiness would take away the dry feeling in the back of my throat.

My legs got a little cramped after a while so I stretched, then I sat again and waited. When the sun fell, I was still alone.

By the third day of waiting a fever had taken over my body – this was not helped by my blanket which wasn't thick enough to keep away the night's chill.

Ayamin was the one thing that kept me moving.

I pulled my blanket and bag down with me. Taking the old guttering one rung at a time. Three rungs down my foot slipped. I tried to cling to the building but my hands were sweating and weak.

Bit by bit they slipped, I found myself falling and next thing I knew, I was on the ground with a shoulder that hurt like hell.

Very carefully I picked myself up. I was crying and sniffling like a three-year-old, I could tell I wasn't really in full control of my body.

When I moved my arm, a pain stabbed through it but I could still twist and move the thing which meant it probably wasn't broken – just bruised.

After clearing away most of the snot and tears I plonked myself down at the church step and slowly began to eat stale bread from the bag.

The bread was hard to swallow and hurt my throat when it went down.

'Excuse moi!'

I looked up and swallowed forcefully – just when I thought things couldn't get any worse – a policeman had shown up.

I held up my hands, sick as I was, I knew there was no way I could outrun the policeman, plus he'd know the town much better than I did. The policeman said something else in French, so I pointed to myself, 'English,' I croaked.

The man rolled his eyes, then sighed, 'Of course you are,' He turned and beckoned to me, 'Follow thanks.'

With a cough, I picked myself, my blanket, and the bag up from the step and trudged behind him. It was still early and there were only store owners in the square so far. Still, most of them watched as I made my walk of shame.

It was ironic really. I'd come all that way, evaded half the Italian police force and I'd been caught by a lone officer in a mountain town in France.

I was led to the door of what looked like a small apartment building across the square from the church.

The policeman knocked three times and waited. While he waited, he looked me up and down, then pointed to my nose, 'Sick?'

I nodded.

The door opened and the old gentleman who'd given me the bread appeared. I wiped my nose and wondered if the church man was some sort of commander. The two men talked in French for a while, the cop kept pointing at me while the old man pointed at the church, he had a bemused look on his face. Eventually, the cop left, and the old man looked both ways before beckoning me inside.

My bag bumped on the doorway as I entered. There was a staircase right in front of us.

'You can leave your bag and blanket down here,' he said, 'And please shut the door, it's rather cold out there.'

As I followed the man up the steps it quickly became apparent that I wasn't entering a police station of any sort.

Instead, I stood in an old bachelor's flat.

The room at the top of the stairs was sparsely decorated; a sofa, coffee table, and bookshelf made up the living room while the smell of tea came from the kitchen.

'I was just brewing a pot when I got Officer Bisset's knock.' the man said.

Pulling out two cups and pouring enough tea for both of us he offered me milk and sugar before pointing out that sitting on the couch beat standing. I took a seat and so did he.

I stared at the cup of tea in my hand. My shoulder hurt like hell. I put the tea down, determined to ask whether I could leave now that I wasn't being arrested.

But the old fogie got there first.

'So... you found sanctuary in, or should I say *on*, the house of God.' He smiled, 'What led you here son?'

I shrugged, unsure of what he wanted me to say. I wasn't going to give him the whole story but....

'A girl,' I said, 'I'm waiting for a girl.'

'Ahh,' The man said, 'I thought it may have been Jesus that led you to our church.'

I laughed, it hurt my throat but it felt good, 'I think even Jesus would be pleased to meet this girl, sir.'

He frowned, but very slowly it turned into a smile, 'Perhaps there is a higher purpose to your coming here.'

The man paused for a long swallow of tea, 'Officer Bisset and I are wondering if you would like to stay in my flat for the next few days,' he gestured around, 'As long as you promise not to steal anything, I'd be glad for the company and...' he pulled back the curtain, 'You even have a view of the church should your good lady arrive.'

I smiled and told him I wouldn't take anything (leaving out the fact there wasn't much worth taking).

'It's done then,' the man said, holding out his hand, 'I'm Graeme.'

I shook it, 'Call me Danny.'

****

The days passed slowly in Graeme's house. I spent most of my time at his window watching the church.

Every few hours Graeme would turn on the kettle and grab two cups from his dish rack.

'How about a cup of tea?'

My answer was always yes. The hot liquid seemed to calm my nerves a little. Graeme wrote letters and we played a bit of chess. Despite the warmth, I think I was more miserable there than on the roof of the church. At least outside I had the cold to distract me.

It was five days after I'd got to Graeme's flat that he started trying to reason with me.

We were playing a game of chess in front of his windows. Every few minutes I'd glance out at the church. A mist hung in the air and tourists wandered about aimlessly between stores.

'See here boy, suppose she doesn't show up, I don't think you'd want to spend the rest of your life here waiting.'

I shrugged; I didn't know what else to do.

Graeme took out my queen, knocking it to the side of the board.

'A lot of people think losing their queen means the game is over. The truth is... the game isn't over until it's over. Sometimes you can play better without it, and of course, there's always the opportunity to get a new queen.'

Graeme paused and checked to see whether his words had any effect. Some small part of me understood him, but the rest of me was screaming for Ayamin. I avoided his eyes by looking out the window.

Out at the church was a girl with a beanie on. She was sitting on the steps like I had been, gazing around like she was looking for someone. My heart sped up... it looked like... *Ayamin.*

'Your move Danny.'

I was still staring out the window. The girl had got to her feet. Started to walk. *What if it's her... you've waited all this time and she's just going to slip away.*

I stood, knocking over the chessboard.

'Hey, Danny!' Graeme called.

I was running. Down the stairs and into the square. The whole way to her I held my breath. I'd been wrong before. I stopped just a few meters away. Her back was to me.

'Ayamin?'

The girl turned and stared at me. I felt like crying. Her clothes looked different than from above. She had a more rounded face than Ayamin.

She asked a question in French – then pointed up to the church.

I shook my head and turned away from her. In the window Graeme stood watching, disappointment hung on his face as he bent to pick up our game from the floor.

The French girl was trying to ask me another question, but I ignored her as I dragged my feet along the cobbled square. I wondered how I'd apologise to Graeme for messing up. I didn't feel like sitting around anymore. I wanted to crawl into a deep dark hole and just lie there for a while. Part of me wondered if I'd ever be okay. The air was cold on my forehead. I had a headache. I realised the French girl wasn't wearing a beanie. The girl I'd seen out the window had a beanie.

'Hey Danny.'

I stopped short and held my breath. Every muscle in my body was taut. In front of me, beanie in hand, stood Ayamin.

****

I must have stared at her for a minute, maybe two, I couldn't figure out if she was really real or I'd just gone insane.

She took a step towards me, 'It isn't easy to make meetings when you have mountains and a border to cros–'

Her sentence didn't finish, she'd said enough to convince me she was legit, I swept her up in a hug that didn't end until her feet left the ground.

'Ayamin.'

'Danny.'

I kept my arms around her as I lowered her. I couldn't believe it. I'd missed the sight, the smell, the feel of her so badly. She was like water in the desert.

Ayamin touched my face, 'You idiot. It's good to see you Danny.'

I held onto her as we stared at each other. My cheeks were warmed as silent tears trickled down them.

'I was starting to think you'd never show up.'

'Honestly... me too.'

She took a step back – she had no tears on her face.

'Ayamin,' I said, 'I'm sorry. If I could turn back time and make things right I would.'

She sniffed; the cold mountain air was making her nose run.

'Three days ago, I was in a jail cell. I was alone and I had nothing to distract me from my thoughts. I realised that maybe you were right not to tell me Danny.'

She hugged her arms to her chest and continued.

'Maybe I wouldn't have wanted to know you.'

Her words hung in the air between us. I wanted to say I was sorry again. I wanted to get on my knees and beg Ayamin to stay with me. But I kept my mouth shut and my feet on the ground. I had nothing to offer her but myself. If she wanted to leave, she was free to go.

'But now,' she said, 'I want to know everything Danny.'

And then she was crying. Her tears slid free. Her arms stretched out, wrapped around me.

Standing in the Briancon street on that cold winter's day.

With Ayamin in my arms.

I knew we'd be okay.

****

We sat on a crumbled stone wall above Briancon. Its stone buildings and wooden houses seemed like miniatures compared to the landscape around them. There, Ayamin began her story.

'I was angry Danny. I hated you a little bit. So I started to walk. I left Milan and I just kept going. We'd spent all our money on the bus so there wasn't much else for me to do.

Three days later I was in some small Italian town. You might've passed through it. It's the one with the statue of Caesar in it. I found a space to sleep under the arches of a community hall and woke up to flashing lights and a policeman shaking me awake. He told me I couldn't sleep there.

He took me to their jail and gave me the best meal I've ever had. It was some sort of a stew his wife made – but the feeling of the heat filling my cold, empty stomach was heaven.

In the morning the policeman said I should apply for refugee status or I'd either stay locked up or be forced to leave the country. I told him I wanted to get to England and he said it was impossible.

Later he came in carrying a radio and set it down on the table next to me. It was playing your interview Danny.

When it had finished he turned the radio off and we stood there watching each other.

We're going to let you out on bail. He told me, *Whatever you do, you've got to stay in this town. Don't even think about travelling to France... that would be very bad... it'd be even worse if you travelled to the place this Danny was talking about and met up with him... That would be very, very bad. You should most definitely not do that.*

Then he gave me our pack and let me go. When I put the bag on, it felt heavier than I remembered. The policeman waved from the front of the station.

So, I started walking again. I missed you Danny. I really did. I wanted that feeling of us taking on the world together.

I found the policeman had loaded my pack full of all kinds of travel food, enough to keep me alive a few days. So I turned my head towards France and I walked and I walked and I slept a little and walked some more. I found Briancon, and I found you Danny.'

As she finished her story Ayamin pulled her tattered copy of *Two Hearts in the French Night* from the bag.

'No wonder it's set here,' she said, 'This is a place for stories.'

She flicked through the book and stopped when she came to a red poppy preserved between its pages. It made me think of Teete.

'Is that her flower?'

'She said she wanted to see Paris. So, I'm going to show her.'

I slipped my hand into Ayamin's.

We walked back through the town to Graeme's flat. He was waiting at the door with a patient, sad smile on his face. Our final cup of tea together was spent talking about the trip ahead.

As we went to leave, he handed me a bag of scones, and a map of France for the road, 'You take care Danny.'

Part of me felt guilty for leaving Graeme so suddenly. But a bigger part was consumed with Ayamin. I shook his hand and we left.

At the side of the church, Henry the scooter sat in a small pile of snow. Ayamin buzzed around him cleaning off his seat, admiring his colour and the pink helmet attached to him.

'He's so cute!!'

'Alright,' I said, 'I'm feeling a little jealous now.'

Ayamin laughed, bent down and kissed his headlight.

'How about n...'

She didn't have time to finish as a snowball exploded on her face. Ayamin screamed and then bent down to gather up a small mountain of snow in her arms.

'Come here.'

She ran after me, I dodged her attack, then leapt on her. The two of us landed face first in a pile of snow.

When she poked her head out from the snow little snowflakes were hanging from her eyelashes. Her face was red.

'Danny!'

I threw my head back and laughed until she shoved a chunk of snow into my mouth.

'Now we're even.'

I wrapped a hand around her butt and slid her body closer to mine. Ayamin was grinning as I kissed her forehead, her nose, and then her lips.

On the surface, her skin was icy and made me shiver.

'Danny,' she whispered.

'Yeah?'

'I'm cold.'

I laughed, and with a groan, stood to my feet. I held out a hand to Ayamin.

'Come on you.'

I pulled Henry's key from my bag and Ayamin hopped on the seat behind me, little Henry's suspension dropped to an all-time low with our combined weight.

'Ready?' I asked, turning the key.

'Ready,' she grinned.

Little Henry started first time, I revved the engine, and we shot through the town square. Ayamin's hair trailed behind her, 'England here we come!'

We streamed down the mountainsides, I felt Ayamin's arms tighten around my chest, she was yelling pure joy.

'I missed you Ayamin.'

'I love you Danny.'

****

We flew through the backroads of France.

Hedges and fields, and flowers and fruits. Little villages dotted the countryside, and we'd catch glimpses of painted murals and stone architecture. The scents of freshly baked bread and coffee being roasted filled the wind. It was a land made for the senses.

The light was golden when I spotted a gap in the hedgerow we'd been following. Ayamin's hands tightened around my waist as we turned into it.

We left tired little Henry parked in the corner of the field while the two of us eased ourselves underneath the hedge.

Once inside the branches formed a little cocoon over us. There was no wind, the sun had made the earth warm, it was almost like being under a blanket.

Ayamin opened our worn pack and pulled out a large square rag. She was smiling.

'I don't think there's a better way to travel France than on the backroads on a little Vespa named Henry.'

She pulled out some plum jam, a pinch of butter, and Graeme's scones and sat them on our little tablecloth.

'Just for a minute,' she said, 'Can we appreciate how perfect this is.'

My stomach was growling, 'Not many people would say that about eating scones under a hedge with a wanted criminal.'

Ayamin smiled as she spread the butter and jam over a slice, 'Some might say you being on the run makes it a little more romantic.'

'Oh yeah?' I raised an eyebrow, 'You know what else is romantic?'

'*What?*'

'Everything about you.'

I kissed her as she laughed. The scone was still in her hand and I got jam all over my cheek. She wiped it off with the edge of our rag-tablecloth.

We ate and we kissed and we ate some more. The dark arrived and Ayamin spread the blankets over us. The night was cold but we were warm.

****

We were in Paris in time for lunch, and what a lunch it was. Little Henry waited faithfully at the bakery we'd stopped at. Fresh croissants steamed in our hands as we wandered the streets, signs for Calis hung overhead, and the sun was out.

'It almost seems surreal,' Ayamin said, 'We're nearly there.'

'Yeah,' I shook my head, 'Sometimes I wonder if I've dreamt the past five months.'

We walked in silence for a while, just taking it all in. At one point I closed my eyes and heard the slight rumble of traffic moving around, the clinking of glasses as café staff collected them, chatter in French, laughter, and the smells of good food, coffee, flowers, and the feel of a slight breeze on my skin.

We saw the Eiffel Tower. Ayamin posed in front of it and I pretended to take pictures of her. That's the one moment where I really wished I still had my phone.

Her eyes and her smile seemed to shimmer with excitement and she couldn't stop laughing.

'Paris!' she shouted, 'Danny! We're in Paris and this is the Eiffel Tower.'

She did a little dance and then leapt onto my back.

'Onwards,' she said, pointing to the Seine River.

We walked down the river through the centre of town and crossed a bridge where couples wrote their names on locks and attached them to the steel railing.

We stopped halfway along the bridge and breathed in. Ayamin's eyes were still shining as she reached up and kissed me. I felt her waist pressed against me and her hair touching my face. She was smiling beneath her kiss.

It took us hours to walk to our final destination – the Notre-Dame. But I savoured every moment. The twin tops of the white stone building stood far above us.

There were guided tours but we couldn't afford them, instead, we wandered around the base of the building, touching the stone that had been worn smooth by thousands of hands before us.

We followed a group of tourists up a set of stairs. They laughed and shouted in their own languages and took pictures every two steps. The noise was so human and so happy and a little girl in pink shoes waved at us. Ayamin waved back.

The staircase led out onto a roof and the city spread out beneath us. The tourists had fallen silent, their cameras were in their pockets and the only sounds were the sounds of the city.

I looked to Ayamin. Her book was lying open in her hands – Teete's red poppy almost shone between the white pages and black text.

Gently she held the poppy up, brought it to her lips and whispered a sentence to it. Her eyes shone, and her fingers trembled slightly as she kissed the flower and then released it off the edge.

The wind caught it, caressed it, and sent it spinning past brick walls, an art gallery, cafes, theatres, and crowds of other people.

We watched as it disappeared into the sunset. A little piece of red sent to join all the oranges, yellows, golds, and blues in the sky.

****

The Paris sun was quickly replaced by halogen street lights. The nightlife began, but now people moved more quickly and in groups. Voices were harsher.

Ayamin held onto my arm as we walked down the street, 'I've never felt as safe sleeping in the cities.'

I nodded, 'There's something about people after dark.'

We stopped walking, one of the side streets in front of us, no more than 200 meters from the Notre-Dame was packed with white and blue tarpaulins.

Children played football in the street, a group of women sat in front of a steaming pot of rice and the men talked with their backs against the walls of the street.

A football bounced towards us. I stuck my leg out, stopped the ball and held it under my foot. A crowd of kids came rushing towards me, stopping only a meter or two in front of us. Some of them had bare feet.

One of the older boys held out his hands. His teeth shone under the streetlights.

I rolled the ball out and hackyed it four times before passing it to him. He grinned. Did five, then passed it back to me. Ayamin was groaning, 'You'll embarrass yourself Danny.'

I kept going anyway. Lifting the ball with my foot, and tapping it with my feet a couple of times before bringing it to my head then back down to make six.

The kids around us yelled and a little boy with two missing front teeth high fived me.

The older boy did seven keepy uppys. I barely managed eight. He rolled the ball onto his bare foot and made a start, reaching seven before the ball appeared to go out of his control, he stumbled for it and got his eighth, all the kids around us gasped but he leapt for the ball and managed nine. I wiped my forehead...

With an easy grin on his face he continued to twenty, then thirty, then forty hackies. The boys in our circle began to crack up laughing and that's when I realised it had never been a contest. We slapped hands. The little kid with no teeth cheered.

Ayamin crouched in front of them, 'Does anyone here speak Arabic?'

The boy I'd been playing against nodded, and so did his little toothless brother.

'What is happening here with all these people in the street?' Ayamin asked.

'We're camping,' said the little boy.

The footballer shrugged, 'It's a tent village,' he tilted his head to the side and eyed the pack on Ayamin's back, 'Anyone is allowed to stay.'

The pair led us to a canvas tent where their father sat reading a mud-smeared National Geographic magazine under the light of the streetlamp.

'Hello brother, hello sister,' he said in a rich, deep voice, 'You've come to stay in the most cultured tent city in the world?'

I glanced at Ayamin, wondering if I should ask about getting to England, but the man seemed to take my look for confusion.

'The world's greatest works of art sit not far from our humble tents,' he said, 'Great plays are performed every night two streets over, and if you're quiet enough you can hear the musicians of tomorrow performing on the other side of this very building.'

He smiled, a dreamy book-like smile, 'But something tells me you won't be staying on our street for very long.'

'We want to get to England,' Ayamin said.

'Are you rich?'

Ayamin shook her head, 'We wouldn't be here if we were.'

He sighed, 'Then I'd say to you, try and claim refugee status in France.'

'But there is a way?'

The man stared at her, there was silence, he almost seemed to be daring her to walk away. After half a minute his eyes dropped, 'The body snatchers charge the least.'

'The body snatchers?'

'Sometimes the people who go in those vans just disappear.'

Ayamin nodded, 'I've heard stories... How do we find them?'

'You don't, you have to gather all the money you can, then wait for them to show up.'

I looked over at Ayamin, then tapped my pocket. She nodded. We both knew we were broke.

'I don't suppose anyone goes as low as fifty euro?' I asked.

The man laughed, 'More like five hundred brother, and that's each. Fifty would barely get you a taxi.'

Ayamin looked at me and grimaced, we both knew what we'd have to do, but it wouldn't be pleasant.

'I guess we could sell Henry,' I said.

Ayamin nodded slowly, 'Poor little Henry.'

'Let's just keep it quiet around him,' I said, 'He won't take it well.'

The man shook our hands. His name was Yamiz. Yamiz the dentist.

****

Henry waited exactly where we'd left him, perfectly oblivious to his fate. We rode him back to the alleyway of tents and gave him a little wash with some rags and water from a leaking tap. We were so scared he'd be stolen that Henry got to sleep his last night in the tent with us.

The next day we wheeled him to a trade-in centre on the edge of the city that had a terrible record of ripping refugees off but wasn't prone to checking for identification.

Ayamin waited in the street as I took the scooter in. The large sliding door to the shop was open. In one corner of the shop sat fifteen Japanese made scooters with hefty price tags attached.

'Hello?' I called out.

The head of a greasy looking man appeared from beneath a car.

'Hey there, you speak English?' I called, 'I've got a trade for you.'

The man wheeled himself out from under the car. He was short, sweaty and his skin was slightly blackened from all the grease in his workshop.

'I've got a scooter here, how much can I get for it?'

He paused for a moment as if deciding whether or not he would talk to me, 'Cash?' he asked.

'Cash.'

The man walked past me and gave Henry's front tire a sharp kick which Henry wouldn't have liked at all. Without pausing to ask he climbed onto Henry's seat, started the engine, and revved the poor little scooter half to death.

This confirms it, I thought, *he's an asshole.*

The man wiped his face with the oily sleeve of his overalls, 'It's a Vespa trash, the engine on this thing will be useless.'

He glanced at me for a moment before shrugging, 'I'll give you two hundred euros to take it off your hands.'

That made my heart sink, no way would we be able to afford the smugglers' fee.

'Actually, I was looking for more like a thousand euros,' I said, 'This Vespa is worth double those imports you're robbing people with.'

The man snorted but couldn't keep a smile from his lips. When dealing with an asshole it can be useful to be an asshole yourself.

'Three hundred,' he said, 'And I give you one jap imports, I can't sell them here.'

'Nine hundred and you can keep your import.'

The man went back to Henry, felt the handlebars, rubbed his hand over a few of the dents in it.

'Listen,' I said, 'I'm in a hurry,' I pointed to Ayamin, 'You see that girl over there? She asked me to sell the scooter. I'm going to say it went for a hundred euros and I'll keep the rest, but you'd better make it worth my while. Eight hundred and fifty or I'm going to the next store.'

The man looked taken aback that I was being so direct, but then he saw Ayamin and his face changed.

'Eight hundred,' he grinned. I paused for a moment, let him think he was getting away with something, then sighed and shook his hand.

I nodded to the little scooter that had carried me so far. Henry had strips of grease on him from where the man had touched him. I hoped he'd find a nice home.

****

Ayamin and I walked back to the camp with four hundred euros each sitting nicely in our pockets. Just as we arrived a charity food van appeared. The refugees around us ran towards it in a stamping of feet and cries in twelve different languages.

Ayamin threw me our bag as she went to claim a spot in the line for us. I pulled a large coat over my head before taking a place next to her. I kept my head down and hidden as we shuffled forwards, occasionally flicking a glance at the lines either side of me.

Seeing the people pressing each other towards the food truck made me think of a random late-night T.V documentary on pigs I'd watched at some point. Whenever the farmer's truck showed up all of the pigs ran to it to receive the farm scraps. Some of the pigs even lined up.

The soup we were given tasted good though, chicken with vegetables, the sort that helps when winter is cold.

****

The next day three smugglers came by. They wore slightly raggedy suits, leather shoes, and one of them smoked as they walked through the camp. The refugees followed them with their eyes, kids peered out from beneath tarpaulins, and even the football stopped bouncing.

The three men went to the centre of the camp. Their eyes swept over it as if they were searching for someone. After two minutes of staring, they nodded to each other.

'Who wants to go to England?'

A young man stepped forward, then another holding his wife with one hand and his kid with the other. All up ten people stepped forwards.

'You need five hundred euros each – children as well,' the smuggler said.

Ayamin looked at me and raised her eyebrow, but I just nodded along with the rest of the refugees.

'We have to try our luck,' I whispered to her, 'Maybe they'll take four hundred?'

'The truck will arrive at the end of the street in ten minutes,' said one of the smugglers, 'Hurry up and grab your stuff.'

Ayamin and I rushed to our bags, although we needn't have hurried, months of travelling had left us well prepared. Our packs were buckled up and ready to go.

I hoisted the larger one onto my back and turned to Ayamin, taking her hand. I started to walk towards the truck but Ayamin stood still.

'Part of me thinks we should stay,' she said, 'I don't think the body snatchers will like being short-changed.'

I shook my head, 'Our situation won't improve sitting in another refugee camp. This is a chance Ayamin. We should take it.'

She glanced at the truck, the first refugees had paid, and one of the smugglers slid under the truck and opened a hatch, 'You crawl under,' he said to them.

Two young men made their way under the truck, they threw their packs through the hole in the middle, then disappeared into the belly of the machine.

'Next,' the man at the front of the line called.

'Decision time,' I said.

Ayamin's face had gone white. I could see the hunger for England in her eyes. That truck represented a new life for her. She was shivering.

'Do you think it'll be safe Danny?'

'I can't tell Aya. But I know if we make it, we'll have a shot at a better life.'

'Okay.'

We were last in line. Ayamin and I presented our piles of cash and the man told us to hop inside.

'Wait,' he said as we reached underneath, 'This is four hundred. Another of the smugglers pulled me out from under the truck, 'You think this is charity?' he said, kicking me, 'We risk our lives to help you.'

'Please,' Ayamin begged, 'We've been travelling for months.'

The man shook his head, 'You a hundred short, each.'

'We will pay when we're in England,' I said.

The man grinned, 'Oh yes you will, you pay very much indeed,' he gave me a shove, 'Get under there.'

I took Ayamin's hand, we clambered under the truck and pushed ourselves through a hole in the floor.

We felt hands helping us as we climbed into a small space that thudded with the sound of the engine.

I reached for Ayamin, when she felt my arm, she latched onto me. Below us the smugglers screwed a steel plate into the hole we'd crawled through. There was a harsh squeaking.

With the space fully enclosed I started to feel a little claustrophobic, it was so dark I could barely see the other refugees, and the only sound that reached our ears was the throbbing, then roaring of the truck's engine as it drove off.

'At least we're not going to drown this time,' Ayamin said.

'Yeah,' I said, holding her, 'There's that I guess.'

After half an hour of twisting and turning, diesel fumes started to enter the space. One of the refugees on the side opposite us vomited when we went over a large bump. His puke sat there, sloshing around. I clutched at my stomach, willing myself not to throw up.

A man who had two dirt-faced kids with him started banging on the walls of the truck.

'We die in here,' he yelled, 'We die.'

'The walls are too thick,' one of the young men yelled, 'They won't hear you.'

'We die,' he screamed, 'We die if we don't get out.'

He flailed his arms, knocking a woman against the opposite wall and tripping over his sobbing snot-nosed kids.

'We die,' he screamed, 'We die, we die, we die.'

Two young men pounced on him and held him on the floor as he threw his arms around. His hair dipped into the puke and he screamed like a dying cat. It took twenty minutes for him to calm down, and the whole time his kids were sobbing. The engine roared, and one of the walls began to heat up until we couldn't touch it any longer.

We swung around a corner at full speed and I bent over. A brown liquid erupted from my mouth. My stomach kept heaving but there was nothing more to throw up. The small brown puddle I'd created swung with the truck. Ayamin's hand was rubbing my back.

'It's okay,' she said, 'It's okay.'

I shook my head, 'We should've waited.'

She took my hand, 'We're here now Danny,' The light in that space was dim, but I could hardly see her eyes, 'Those men aren't going to let us go.'

I shuddered, 'I know, but I'm going to fight them.'

She was looking at me, I was looking at her. Blood dribbled down her cheek from a scratch. There was grease in her hair. She was almost calm.

'People are scared of us Danny. They're scared because we're poor. Because they think we're taking what they've been given.

They should be scared because no matter what desires are in their hearts, they can't be stronger than that crying man over there and his desire to see his kids have a better life. That's why we're going to survive this. No matter what comes next.'

The refugees stared at her. They were dirty, starving, bloodied, and bruised, but their ears still worked.

Four words were spoken by those refugees. They were four words I'd never heard before, and four words that I can't properly translate. But the Syrians, and the Afghans and the Somalians began to chant them. They bashed their fists and their feet against the sides of the truck as they spoke, creating a beat that resounded through the truck.

The truck stopped and the chanting died away. A metallic tapping sound started. One of the women screamed for help.

We all listened. A scraping sound came from underneath us. More of the refugees were shouting. The small space echoed the voices. A patch of the floor started to turn.

A searchlight appeared and so did a head, the light shone round and the head began cursing. For the first time in a long time, I heard the Yorkshire accent.

'Bloody hell, I've found them.'

****

The ten of us sat in a line at the United Kingdom border security office breathing in the sweet scent of purified air.

Joy and uncertainty moved through the room. *We're in England!* But also, w*hat happens to us now?*

Still, things weren't all bad. After being asked our name and having our photographs taken we were led into a shower block by a middle-aged Arabic woman.

'If you wish to clean yourself,' she said, eying up the flecks of dirt, puke, and blood on our skin, 'Now is the time to do so.'

I stepped into a cubicle and stripped quickly, the smell of diesel and spew began to disappear as I washed. I only allowed myself a moment to enjoy the hot water hitting my skin before I tried to think ahead. We were going to be questioned. I needed a story. A good one, and somehow, I needed to explain that story to Ayamin.

'Hey Ayamin,' I called.

She was in the cubicle next to me, 'What will we say?' she asked in Arabic.

'I've got no plan.'

For a couple of minutes, there were only the sounds of water running, and we were nearing the end of our showering time when Ayamin spoke again.

'If they don't recognise you,' she said, 'Then we'll say you came from Syria as well... You grew up in Damascus in a small townhouse and your parents – *no* grandparents looked after you until you were sixteen when the three of you were taken by Islamic State. You escaped, with the help of your granddad, fled to the refugee camp in the south of Turkey and stayed there until you met me.'

I nodded, the showers were beginning to turn cold, 'And from there we can keep our stories basically the same.'

I dried off and threw on the grey top and sweatpants that had been provided for us. The feel of soft clean clothes on my skin was surreal.

We wandered back to the holding cells and sat down. Ayamin leant her head on my shoulder as one by one the refugees disappeared into the 'interview rooms'.

I asked the woman who'd shown us the showers what happened in the interview rooms.

'They hear your story, ask questions, then set up a court date.'

I wrapped my arms around Ayamin and closed my eyes for a second. The shower had left my muscles feeling like jelly. We'd been on the road for months. I almost fell asleep as she curled into me.

It took two hours for them to reach us, by that time all the other refugees had been interviewed and taken somewhere else in the building.

A muscular security guard came into the waiting room. He mumbled to the woman looking after us who raised an eyebrow then walked over to Ayamin, 'It is time to go.'

Ayamin sat up and squeezed my hand, 'I'll see you soon,' she said.

I nodded.

****

I was left with the tall muscular guard who'd come in. At first, my thoughts were consumed with Ayamin but as time went on, I started to get uncomfortable under the man's gaze.

I waited for an hour, then two, and I had nothing to do except bite my nails. Ayamin had been in the interview room for too long.

I tried to breathe deep as the muscular guard's radio flared to life, he mumbled something into it which I couldn't catch and then walked over to me.

'Time for your interview.'

I followed him down a long grey corridor to a stainless-steel door. Through the door sat an immigration officer. Leaning against one wall was the woman who'd shown us the showers, she was the only one in the room who seemed to have any emotion.

The man pointed to a chair opposite him, 'Sit down.'

I sat. The chair was slightly warm - it hadn't been long since Ayamin had finished. There was a steel table between me and the officer. On it sat two glasses of water.

'Tell us your name,' the officer said.

'I'm Danny,' I said, then turned to the woman, 'Do you mind if we use Arabic?'

She translated it for the officer who just shook his head, 'Danny Frey, we know who you are, we know you're wanted by the police, and we know the story you made up in the shower. Don't waste our time. We're here to listen to your story and decide how best to deal with you, don't try to lie to us, don't try to mislead us.'

He waited for a response from me, I just sat there, any hopes I had slowly sunk away.

The man leaned in a little, 'Why did you leave the refugee camp Danny? And why are you trying to get back to England?'

I stared at his face, gaunt and hard, he'd probably done the same job hundreds and hundreds of times.

'I have a short answer and a long answer for you.'

The man snorted, 'What's the short one?'

I looked towards the door, and felt the edge of the seat.

'There was a girl.'

Behind him, the Arabic woman laughed. The officer was suppressing what I could only assume was a smile.

'And the long answer?' asked the man, a little kinder this time.

'The long answer...' I picked up one of the glasses and took a sip, 'The long answer begins in England.'

****

The trial was set for two weeks from the day we'd been found. It was a quick turnaround as far as the legal system was concerned, but then again there wasn't much to Ayamin's case.

They had to decide whether she would be allowed to stay in England and claim refugee status, or whether she'd be sent 'back' to where she came from – although no one was entirely sure where that was.

While having a roof over my head was great at first, I got progressively lonelier and more bored over the first two days in my cell. My guard only spoke in two-word bursts, but sadly these short conversations were the highlight of my day.

The guard pulled open a screen on my door.

'Visitor's coming.'

I sat up on my bed, saw his face and dull eyes peering at me from behind the screen, 'What?'

He sighed as if the extra words were a burden, 'A visitor – wants to – see you.'

'Is it Ayamin?' I asked.

The man just shrugged, 'Can't say.'

'When's she coming?'

'Midday tomorrow.'

As I went to ask another question the screen slid back into place. I shrugged and lay back on my bed, it had to be Ayamin, *who else would want to see me?*

That night I dreamt about a rural English road, complete with hedgerows, and little robins flying about. I imagined the two of us walking along it, the pack sitting high on my back. We picked dark blackberries and raspberries and ate them and talked.

It's funny the things you miss, there had been so many times where I'd wished that we could at least stay somewhere warm for a night.

Yet there I was dreaming about the road once more.

****

I woke early – a big mistake. After a yawn, I did some push ups, some squats and was able to get five lunges in across my cell. I thought that maybe when I was out, I'd start a petition for border security offices to get board games or a weights machine.

Midday came around slowly. I waited on the floor with my legs crossed like I was back in school. Eventually, my guard knocked on the door and uttered a solemn, 'Stand up.'

I followed him down the corridor. A grin swept my face. The guard pulled open the door of a meeting room and held it open.

'Don't be – too long,' he said.

I walked into the room. The door closed with a metallic squeak behind me and the smile fell from my face.

There, sitting on the opposite chair was Judge Streisand – the same woman who had decided I should go to Syria.

I stared at her, not quite believing what I was seeing.

She gave a courtroom smile, 'Hello Danny.'

There was a seat in front of me, I fumbled my way into it and breathed out a sigh, 'You're the last person I was expecting.'

Streisand grinned for a moment, then her face took on a business-like look.

'From what I hear you've had quite an adventure.'

'You can say that again.'

'And look where it's left you now.' She gestured to the metal walls around her, 'Was it worth it Danny? All that trouble you've caused, the money that's been spent trying to find you, the hundreds of newspapers and television screens with your face on them. Does it feel like it's worth it?'

I stared at her face; it was older than I remembered it. I could see wrinkles there, or maybe it was just that the light in court was less intense. I nodded my head.

'It was worth it.'

'Explain that to me....'

I leant back and ran a hand through my hair

'From as far back as I can remember I've sort of wandered through life. You saw me. I had no purpose.'

I took a sip of water from the cup beside me.

'With Ayamin I suddenly had a direction for my energy and my thoughts. I was helping this girl reach her dream, even if part of that dream was the shitty London suburbs I grew up in.' I held out my hands, 'So what if I go to jail, I was heading there anyway. At least now I have a good reason for being locked up.'

Streisand stared at me in silence. My throat was feeling raspy again and I took another sip of the water.

'I spoke to Donna before I came over,' Streisand said, 'She's doing okay, but it's hard finding another job.'

I went to speak but Streisand held up her hand, 'She lost her job because of your little stunt... These things you've done have a wider reach than you could possibly imagine.'

I lowered my head a little, imagining the sweet woman who'd looked after us standing in line for an unemployment cheque. The thought wasn't a nice one.

Streisand took a deep breath, 'Still, I think if it was her sitting in front of you right now instead of me, she'd forgive you if she heard what you'd said.'

The judge's face lightened, 'It doesn't make much sense to me, but Donna said she cried when she listened to your radio interview – and I imagine she wasn't the only one.'

I cocked my head as Streisand continued.

'You may not realise it just yet, but both you and Ayamin have attained celebrity status. In just under two weeks her fate is to be decided in court,' she pulled up a list of names on her phone, 'I called in there on my way to see you and all of the media spots have been booked out. Whatever happens to Ayamin the world will be watching.'

'They have to let her stay then, don't they?' I asked, 'She just wants to live here.'

Streisand shook her head, 'Not all publicity is good publicity. This trial's got very political.'

I scrolled through the list – there were big names. The BBC, Guardian, CNN.

'There are people saying it's a good lesson on why we should have open borders, while others argue that the public interest shouldn't sway the result and that she's been known to associate with criminals, namely yourself.'

I blinked, 'What can I do?'

'You can't do a thing – at least not in this cell... but speaking with you today I can see your heart is in the right place Danny,' she nodded to me, 'I will not help you with your own trial, as far as I'm concerned you deserve what you get – but I will help you with Ayamin.'

She glanced at the door of the interview room and back at me, 'Do you pray Danny?'

'What? Oh... no, not really.'

'Well, maybe it's time you start... There's a chapel here. Inmates can use it on Sundays at around midday...' she winked, 'Maybe you should give it a go.'

'I will.'

I reached over the table to hug her. Streisand went rigid, but eventually, she wrapped her arms around me.

'Why?' I asked, 'Why are you helping her?'

Streisand stepped back, straightened her jacket, then held up her finger, 'This is not to be repeated to anyone, ever.'

She looked into my eyes and sighed, 'Because maybe I was one of the people who cried during your radio interview.'

****

It was another four days before I saw anyone. In that time, I had twelve meals, did 384 push ups, countless lunges, and worried like crazy.

Sunday arrived, and sure enough, I was able to visit the chapel.

Kneeling in front of the cross reminded me of Graeme and Briancon. I thought about waiting at the church there and how I always seemed to be waiting for Ayamin.

I felt a faint breeze on the back of my neck as the chapel door opened. *It's my guard,* I thought and kept staring up at the cross, trying to prolong my time away from the cell.

The footsteps stopped beside me... They didn't sound like the guard's boots.

'I've been looking for you.'

The familiar voice shocked me to my feet. When I spun it was Donna.

The former Red Cross leader seemed to have shrunk since I'd seen her last. She had dark patches around her eyes, and her skin seemed pale.

'So...' she said, her tone hard, bordering on bitter, 'You were coming back to England all along.'

'I'm sorry,' I backed away a step, 'I shouldn't have left – at least not the way I did.'

'We looked for you for months Danny, the police forces of five countries helped search for you.'

'I'm sorry,' I repeated, 'I wish it had been different.'

'You left for some girl,' she held her hands in the air, 'For love??'

I watched as her mouth moved into a smile.

'I was more worried than angry Danny.' She shook her head, 'You're young. You did something stupid for a good reason.'

From her pocket, she pulled out a small black box and flipped it open. Inside was a diamond ring that seemed to shine in the chapel light.

I shifted my gaze from the ring to Donna, and back to the ring again.

'It's mine,' Donna whispered, 'It's been ten years since my hubby passed away,' she pulled the ring from its box, and studied it, 'This lump of metal hasn't seen the light very much since then... but in ten minutes we're going to use it to help save Ayamin.'

Donna looked at me and held out the ring.

'This is your choice Danny – but the judge for Ayamin's case is hard on migrants. Her being married to a citizen could be the best shot we have of keeping her in the country.'

The diamond flashed in the light.

'Woah... that's the plan?'

She nodded, 'We're not certain it can save her. But it's all we've got.'

'I wish I could've proposed properly,' I said, 'She deserves better.'

I reached out and took the ring. The moment it was in my hand Donna wrapped me up in a bear hug.

'You both do,' she said, 'You both deserve so much more.'

The emotion in her voice made my throat go dry. Her hands were warm on my back and I felt like other kids must feel when they hug their mum. All sense of toughness disappeared. My legs felt weak.

The doors to the chapel flew open, and Judge Streisand's voice cut through the space, 'We are running behind schedule.'

I stepped back from Donna and looked to Streisand, next to her stood Ayamin.

Ayamin looked like a pale crying angel.

I ran. She met me in the middle. Our arms locked around each other. Her face felt just right as it brushed mine. My hands clung to her.

'Alright... alright...' Judge Streisand said with just a hint of a smile, 'If we hang around too long the guards will start to think we're up to something.'

She marched to the front of the chapel and pulled out two pieces of paper from the book under her arm. Ayamin took one, I got the other.

'Sign these – they're supposed to be done after the marriage, but I've got a feeling we won't have time.'

As I scrawled my details across the form, I snuck a glance at Ayamin.

'How are you doing?'

She shrugged, kept her pen in motion.

'I miss you Danny, god I'm lonely.'

'Me too,' I breathed in... 'I really wish we could do this properly.'

She nodded and lifted her eyes to mine.

'This might not be enough to let me stay. By next week I could be sent to another country. It's not the way most marriages go, but Danny I'm going to try make the most of it.'

She reached out and held my hand. Her arm shook slightly.

'I love you Danny.'

'I love you Ayamin.'

Streisand took our signed sheets and flipped open her book.

'Dearly beloved, we are gathered here today...'

Judge Streisand moved through the wedding like a steamroller. Her court skills seemed to come to the forefront. Half an hour later and Ayamin was kissing me as we left the chapel. She was crying, I was crying, Donna was crying.

I swear Streisand wiped away a tear as she reminded everyone that unless we stopped blabbering the plan would be discovered.

'Keep your hands in your pockets when you're walking to court, and for goodness sake try not to give the guards any indication.'

We all nodded, and still Ayamin clung to me. Her grip was so strong and yet so frail all at the same time. As we held each other I ran my thumb along her cheek, wiping away the tears that sat there.

'We're going to be okay Ayamin,' I said, 'And when all of this is done. We'll be free.'

She pushed her forehead into my chest and cried some more. I kissed the top of her head as my throat turned dry and tears slid down my cheeks.

Then the guards were there, splitting us apart, and telling Judge Streisand and Donna that their time was up and they needed to leave, NOW.

'I love you Danny,' Ayamin called as we were walked our separate ways.

****

The rest of the week was hell. The moment my guards left I began to cry. At first, I cried because of Ayamin and the fact I'd been able to touch and hold her, then I cried because I wouldn't see her until the trial.

Days passed slowly, by the fourth I'd walked 12,000 paces, done 253 push ups and 706 squats. I was bored, and I was worrying.

In my life I'd never been depressed before. But in those three days leading up to the trial, I stopped eating, I couldn't sleep. All I could think about was Ayamin's face. What it would look like if her dreams were crushed. I thought about never seeing her again. I had no idea where they'd take her if she was barred entry.

It seemed everything we'd been working to achieve over the past few months had been for nothing. All that walking, fighting, and surviving.

I wanted to die. But also, I wanted to see Ayamin again. Our plan gave me one sliver of hope. It wasn't much, but it was enough.

****

On the day of Ayamin's trial, I woke up beside the toilet. Bits of spew flecked the toilet bowl from where I'd thrown up the night before.

'English food,' I groaned, 'Oh how I've missed you.'

As wrinkled pieces of potato disappeared down the drain, I rested my hands on my knees and took a good look at myself in the bathroom tiles.

I've broken the law and almost been to juvie, I've travelled far, worked in a hospital, and fallen in love. I've crossed the Aegean on a life-raft, stolen lemoni in Greece, snuck into Macedonia, and ridden freight trains through the night.

I'll probably never finish high school, I can work well with my hands, and after this, I'll have at least half a year in jail to decide what sort of job I want when I get out.

I'd lived a bloody good life over the last couple months and after everything I'd been through the thought of jail didn't scare me the way it once had. I knew who I was and what I believed in.

The only thing that matters to me at this moment is whether Ayamin is allowed into the country – that's what I'm going to tell the judge today.

****

Just after 10am the guards led me to an interview room in handcuffs.

The room was small. A large TV and camera took up one half, while a desk and two chairs took up the other.

A young woman wearing a blazer and a strained but cheerful smile sat on the chair closest to me.

She gave me her chair, 'It's good to finally meet you, I'm Estelle and I'm acting as an assistant to Ayamin's lawyer. I'm just here to make sure it all goes smoothly for you, as you won't actually be in court today.

I glanced at the camera setup while the guards took my handcuffs off, 'No one told me that.'

Estelle shrugged, 'From what I gathered it had something to do with your history of evading people that want to find you.'

She pressed a button and the screen flicked on – we had a full view of the courtroom and all the people in it.

A Union Jack sat behind the still-empty judge's desk. The public gallery was so packed with cameras and journalists that they nearly spilled out into the area where the legal teams sat.

Sitting on a wooden bench in the thick of it all was Ayamin. Her face seemed calm as her lawyer spoke to her, but I could see her eyes darting around the courtroom.

I don't know whether it was the screen or the lighting or what but her hair seemed almost grey.

'Hello Aya,' I whispered to her.

Ayamin raised her hand and waved – but not to me. Donna entered the screen, she hugged Ayamin and spoke to her. Streisand was there too, she pointed to the camera Estelle and I were watching through as she spoke to Ayamin.

Estelle tapped a red button on the desk in front of us.

'Just so we're on the same page, we've decided if Ayamin's case is going well you'll only have to give a brief statement,' she said.

I lifted my left hand. On it sat the wedding ring, 'You know about this right?'

The lawyer grimaced as she nodded, 'That's what we're worried about. We don't know how the judge will react – especially because no one told her about it. We're going to try to push with the refugee angle and only bring up your marriage as a last resort, sound okay?'

I shrugged, 'You're the lawyer.'

Estelle stared at me, her mouth was open like she wanted to say something more, but then the judge appeared on screen and we turned away from each other.

Estelle glanced at her watch.

'Exactly ten-thirty.'

Even the judge's footsteps, *firm, measured, and deliberate,* let you know she was in control. By the time she sat down the entire room was silent. The judge paused. Cleared her throat, and declared court open.

'Usually immigration cases only take a few hours for us to settle. But the amount of evidence put forward by both sides, and the overwhelming public interest makes it necessary to stretch our court time to an entire day,' the judge glanced up at the rows of journalists and photographers.

'But the law must come first. In every other way, this hearing will be no different to the hundreds of similar cases this court hears every year.'

I found myself watching a suited man sitting at the bench opposite Ayamin. The man's face was like a bulldog, his body too. He had a pen in his hand and as the judge spoke the pen tapped a rhythm on the yellow legal pad in front of him.

The pen stopped moving and his head shifted ninety degrees to stare at me.

I flinched, then felt Estelle's hand on my arm.

'He can't actually see you,' she said.

'That is one scary dude.'

'I know,' she bit her lip, 'That's the opposition lawyer.'

The man kept staring right through me until Ayamin's lawyer began to speak. As the bulldog man's eyes left us I heard Estelle let out a small sigh of relief.

Ayamin's lawyer wasn't nearly as scary. He was a lanky man wearing a lanky jacket, who spoke quickly and nodded to Ayamin every time he mentioned her name.

He wrapped up his remarks and called on Ayamin to speak.

The entire court leaned forwards as she stood up and walked to the stand. Somehow, she managed to look calm and composed. She even managed to smile at the judge as she gave her name.

'I'm Ayamin Yacoub.'

Her lawyer was still on his feet, 'Ayamin's going to read a short summary of her journey to England.'

I watched her face as she read. I'd lived through a decent portion of her tale, but it was interesting to hear the things that were most important to her – Grandma Teete and the stars, the boat ride to Greece, our stay at the Macedonian border, she talked about Italy and France and how much England meant to her.

'Why?' Her lawyer asked, 'Why does England mean so much?'

'Because to me the United Kingdom means safety, it means I can stop being a refugee and start living like a normal person. I can get a job, go to school, sleep in a real bed.'

Her lawyer nodded, 'If Ayamin is allowed to stay she wants to train as a nurse,' he paused and glanced around the courtroom, 'She wants to care for people.'

With a nod to Ayamin, he took a seat. On the bench opposite him, the bulldog lawyer got to his feet. He cleared his throat before he spoke to Ayamin.

'There are many lawyers who'd doubt your story, who'd try to pick at the threads in hopes of unravelling it. But the way you speak makes it clear you'd been through a lot Ms Yacoub. I just want to talk about a few details.'

He tapped his pen on the yellow paper in front of him.

'Firstly, when you boarded the smuggler's truck did you know you'd be entering England illegally?'

'Yes – but we were desperate.'

'Desperate? Can you elaborate on that?'

Ayamin's face went a little red, 'We were living on the street under a leaking tent. We were so poor we went with smugglers that were known to be human traffickers and we still could not afford their full fee...'

The bulldog nodded, 'And if you were so desperate why didn't you consider claiming refugee status in France? Or Italy, Greece, Austria, maybe even Germany? Surely that would've been better than dealing with human traffickers?'

Ayamin opened her mouth but seemed to freeze halfway.

Next to me, Estelle shook her head, 'That man never takes it easy.'

'Is this going to hurt her case?' I asked.

'Depends on what she says – and remember – this guy is only getting warmed up.'

We stared at each other, I felt the ring on my finger and gave it a twist. *Will we need it?*

Ayamin began to speak again and we turned back to the screen.

'I think I just knew more about England... The refugees that talked about it said it was safe – that there were lots of opportunities for the future.'

'And I'm sure many of those other countries offered the same opportunities.' the lawyer scratched his chin, 'Are you aware that in England we have a refugee quota?'

'It's all they seemed to talk about when I saw myself on the news.'

There was a muffled laugh from the media section, even the bulldog seemed to smile,

'Our country can only take so many refugees at once, otherwise, our hospitals, schools, and other services would be overburdened. Our quota for this year is full.

Why should we let you in when there are other refugees – just as needy who have gone through the proper legal processes? Why should they miss out?'

Ayamin's lawyer shot to his feet, 'That's not a fai-'

'No,' Ayamin shouted over top of him.

Her lawyer stopped talking and looked over at her, but her eyes were focused on the bulldog. Her lawyer took a seat.

'I was in the refugee camp for two years. The whole time my Teete and I were trying to do things the 'proper legal way' but no one wanted her. She was too old, too frail, too Syrian.'

Ayamin narrowed her eyes at the bulldog lawyer.

'If somewhere had taken her in she'd still be here today. I tried to follow the laws as best I could, but when a bomb has fallen on your home there's only one law that matters to you and that's the law of survival.'

As Ayamin finished she levelled her stare at the bulldog. He didn't look away.

'Is that all Counsel Draper?' the judge asked.

The bulldog lawyer broke his stare-off with Ayamin and forced a smile, 'That's all.'

'I don't have any questions for you,' the judge said to Ayamin, 'But I want to acknowledge your bravery both today and in your young life so far... You can return to your seat.'

Ayamin nodded and left the stand.

'Woah... that is some girl,' Estelle said, 'No one stares down old Draper like that.'

I grinned, Ayamin's face was calm, her eyes found the camera and she nodded to us.

'That little speech the judge gave about the things Ayamin's been through...' Estelle said, 'That's good for us as well. As long as the Red Cross woman holds up we should be home free.'

Donna was the last person up before lunch. Both lawyers asked about her impression of Ayamin in the refugee camp.

How would you describe Ms Yacoub?

- Kind and bright.

Did she ever cause any trouble?

- No.

How would you describe the conditions at the camp?

- Well, you've seen the pictures... it isn't exactly Buckingham Palace.

Draper the bulldog seemed to have lost his bite. He hardly looked at Donna as he asked two questions that led nowhere.

Lunchbreak was called at quarter past twelve.

'We shall resume at exactly quarter to one,' the judge said and we stood as she left. Ayamin and her lawyer turned and walked out of the court. Estelle's phone started buzzing.

'Time to discuss tactics,' she said as she put it to her ear, 'Counsel McCurdy, good stuff out there.'

While Ayamin's lawyer spoke, I stared at Draper on the T.V screen. He sat at his desk reading through the sheets of paper in front of him.

His shoulders seemed slumped, and his eyes wandered across the pages.

Estelle moved the phone away from her mouth and waved to me.

'We're going to keep your stand as short as possible okay Danny? – And no mention of the marriage.'

I nodded and she put the phone back to her mouth, 'Yep, Danny understands... I know... she did so well!'

On screen one of the bulldog's assistants hurried into view. He mopped at his forehead as he stopped at Draper's desk and put down a sheet of paper.

Draper glanced at it, looked back to his notes, then his eyes sprung open and he seized the paper with both hands.

His arms made quick gestures as he spoke with his assistant. He grinned, picked up his mobile and called someone.

'Hey Danny,' Estelle said, touching my shoulder, 'Ayamin's on the phone.'

She held out her mobile. I placed it to my ear and looked away from the screen.

'Hey Danny,' Ayamin said.

'Hey Aya... Well done out there.'

She laughed, I imagined she shrugged as well, 'I just told myself it wasn't as bad as waiting at the Macedonian border – at least this time I had a full stomach.'

'And I promise, I'm not about to throw you in a creek.'

Ayamin groaned, 'Thanks a lot,' there was a slight pause before she spoke again, but when she did her voice was softer, 'Seriously, thank you Danny... I wouldn't have got past the border without you. I wouldn't have kept walking if you weren't carrying the bag and making lame jokes... I wouldn't be in England if you hadn't been with me in Hungary, or Austria, or Italy, or France, or Turkey...' A sob broke through the phone, and I felt my throat run dry. There was a rustling as Ayamin wiped her eyes, 'The lawyers think we're going to win, and when I'm free I know the one thing I want more than anything – and that's you Danny. I came all this way when the thing I wanted most was right beside me.'

She cried some more, and my voice broke as I spoke, 'They really think you're going to win?'

I could hear her nodding on the other end, 'They do.'

Estelle tapped me on the shoulder, she gestured for her phone.

I held up a finger, lowered the phone, and mouthed *one minute?* Estelle shook her head. I put the phone back to my mouth, 'Aya, I love you so much. Estelle needs her phone back.'

Ayamin sighed, 'Yeah... I know... Good luck out there Danny. I love you.'

I handed the phone back to Estelle, she started speaking to McCurdy again.

The phone call left me a little dazed. As I stared at the screens in front of me, I couldn't stop thinking about Ayamin. It took me a while to realise that the courtroom was empty.

Draper had gone.

****

Estelle got off the phone just before lunch ended, and moments later Ayamin and her lawyer were in the courtroom.

Draper was already sitting, there were two new men seated at his desk. They wore uniforms almost like a police officer's, but I couldn't recognise their faces.

By quarter to one, the entire court was standing as they waited for the judge to appear.

'You're first up Danny,' Estelle said, 'It's pretty simple, you'll tell the judge your name, swear an oath, answer three questions from our side, and then a few from Draper. You'll need to be wary of him, don't go into too much detail unless he asks you to.'

'Sweet.'

We remained standing, as did the rest of the court.

Estelle glanced down at her phone, 'Huh?'

I looked across, 'What is it?'

She showed me her phone screen, 'It's almost one o'clock. The judge is *never* late'

The longer we stood the more agitated Ayamin's lawyer got. I could see McCurdy tapping his foot beneath his desk. He kept ruffling his papers, ordering, and then reordering them.

By contrast, Draper was chatting with the men at his bench. He glanced up at our camera and gave a smile.

The judge entered. Her footsteps were quicker than before. She reached her desk and stared around the courtroom. Her eyes fell on Draper. He nodded.

'Be seated,' the judge said.

There was a ruffle of clothes, then silence as she picked up her pen.

'Over the lunchbreak I received a request from counsel Draper to have our next witness, Mr Danny Frey, appear in court rather than via video – I am now granting this request.'

Ayamin's lawyer leapt to his feet, 'I'm sorry, but surely the request could've been made in open court?'

The judge nodded, 'I don't like granting requests made outside of court. It's not the way justice should work. BUT you have forced my hand counsel McCurdy, why on earth didn't you tell me they were married?'

McCurdy went pale. He dropped one hand to his desk, as if to brace himself.

'I – I – I thought it'd be best to focus on the other areas of Mrs Yacoub's life. They were married without my knowledge – or advice... after the legal process had started. I think they believed it would help Ayamin's case. I believed otherwise.'

The judge gave a bitter laugh, 'It sounds like one mistake after another. Do you have a copy of the marriage certificate with you?'

McCurdy fumbled through a stack of paper until he came to our marriage certificate. He handed it to one of the judge's aides.

Opposite him, the bulldog was grinning. He made a joke to one of the policemen next to him, then stood up.

'Your honour, one of my Italian colleagues has offered to speak while we wait for Mr Frey to arrive.'

The judge paused, then nodded, 'Tell him to take the stand,' then she looked directly at me, 'See you very soon Mr Frey.'

****

'Oh hell,' Estelle said, 'They're using it against us.'

'Who are the Italian guys?' I asked.

'You don't recognise them? Maybe you'll get a better look in court,' Estelle pushed back her chair and stood, 'Let's go meet our maker.'

A guard was waiting for me at the door. I held out my hands behind me for the handcuffs dangling from his belt.

With the handcuffs in place, he led us to a waiting police car. With its light blaring we sped through the London traffic.

Estelle was biting her nails as she stared out at the cars flashing past the window.

I nudged her arm with an elbow, 'What should I say when I get in there?'

She smiled at me, it was a sad smile, 'Just tell them the truth Danny. The truth's all we've got left.'

'That's okay.' I said, when really I meant the opposite. I wanted to tell her I'd do anything to help Ayamin stay here.

Estelle was staring into my eyes. She seemed to understand.

'I listened to your interview Danny, the one at the Italian radio station. You kids have been through a lot. I'm sorry this system is the way it is. I'm sorry we couldn't make it easier for you.'

Our police car pulled up outside the court. I wanted to hug Estelle, but my arms were still handcuffed. Outside the tinted windows, I saw flashes of light. A tear spilled down my cheek. Estelle used the sleeve of her shirt to wipe it away.

'Let's do it for Ayamin,' she said.

I sucked in a final breath, 'For Ayamin.'

****

A shockwave of noise and light hit us the moment we stepped onto the footpath.

It was raining – a proper British downpour – and the reporters who'd been huddling in the court entrance swirled around us.

Estelle grabbed my arm as a microphone was thrust into my face. A flash went off and questions bubbled from their mouths.

We made it through the entrance. Two security guys guided me down the hallway and into an office.

'The crows are hungry today,' one of them said, 'You okay buddy?'

I looked up at him. He was a young guy, not much older than me. his skin reminded me of Ayamin.

'Yeah. I'm okay.'

'They want us to keep you here until the Italians are finished talking.'

'Are they policemen?'

The guy laughed, 'They're traffic cops – apparently they didn't like what you and your missus did to their van.'

Oh...' I laughed, 'That wasn't us though, you see we had a flat tyre in a bunch of lavender fields...'

'Hey,' the guy held up his hands, 'I'm just a guard, you don't need to explain anything to me.'

So Estelle and I sat there, it might've been five minutes, but it felt like an hour.

Finally, a crackling sound came from the younger guy's walkie-talkie.

'Okay Gus, bring them in.'

Estelle helped me to my feet, then the two security guards grabbed an arm each, took me back into the hallway and led me through the two large oak doors at the end of it.

The courtroom was massive in person. Everything seemed to be made of oak or portraits of the Queen.

The guards led me to the stand, then backed off a step or two.

'Mr Danny Frey,' said the judge, so loud it almost hurt my ears, 'There seems to be no end to the trouble you've caused...'

Just a few metres away from me sat Ayamin. I grinned and tried to wave my hands awkwardly from behind my back. She rolled her eyes, but she was laughing as well.

'Mr Frey,' The judge half-yelled, 'Would you please look at me when I'm speaking to you?'

I tore my eyes away from Ayamin, but ended up wishing I hadn't. The judge was old and angry. I much preferred looking at Ayamin.

'Mr Frey, you're our final witness to Mrs Yacoub's character and actions – what you say could be *very meaningful* to this case.'

I nodded.

'Well then, say your oath and Counsel McCurdy can begin.'

I glanced at Estelle.

'I solemnly swear to tell the truth, the whole truth and nothing but the truth.'

Estelle nodded, and next to her McCurdy began his questions.

'Mr Frey,' he said, then gave a slight cough to clear his throat, 'I want to start with the thing that is no doubt on everyone's mind – the marriage...' McCurdy glanced at the bulldog, whose face was like a chess player's – blank, yet in control of the situation. McCurdy seemed to pale a little.

'The marriage... Am I right in saying that you and Mrs Yacoub are in love?'

I nodded, 'Yes.'

'Had you thought about marrying Mrs Yacoub before you arrived in the United Kingdom.'

I thought back to the church in Briancon, arriving there on Henry the Vespa – I'd thought about getting married then.

'Yes! I had.'

'So am I right in saying that you didn't so much get married because of the trial – but brought the marriage forwards.'

'I guess... yeah.'

Draper – the bulldog had the corners of his lips curled upwards. He jotted down something on his yellow legal pad, then glanced back up at McCurdy who took a sip of water before beginning his next question.

'Why should Mrs Yacoub be allowed into the country?'

'Because she's been through so much already. She's worked harder to get here than anyone in this courtroom, and because when she's here she'll make the United Kingdom a better place to live. She cares about people, she wants to work and earn her keep, she's kind.'

McCurdy glanced at Draper a final time, then nodded to me, 'That's all the questions I have. Thank you Danny.'

The room's attention turned to Draper who moved smoothly to his feet, the same way a spider might as it gets ready to spring. His eyes were firmly on me, sizing me up, searching for clues in my movements.

'Mr Frey...' He paused, and without realising it I began to lean forwards, like an insect into his web.

'Danny, I'm going to ask the same questions as my learned colleague McCurdy – only I'm going to ask them with a little more detail, I'm going to find out what you actually mean when you say *I guess*.'

The judge cleared her throat, 'I'd like to remind you all that we do not tolerate personal attacks in this courtroom – I'm not reprimanding you Counsel Draper – but you did come very close. You may continue.'

Draper nodded; he was barely trying to hide his smile.

'Why did you marry Mrs Yacoub?'

'Because I love her, and because I want her to stay in the country.'

He raised an eyebrow, and leaned forwards, over his desk. I decided then that court is unfair. He was in his element – a little king of the courtroom. I wondered how things would be different if we were sitting in a muddy tent – or met on the road.

'Did anyone tell you,' he said, pausing between each word, 'That marriage is about more than just swapping rings. If you do it properly it's life-long.'

I felt my cheeks start to heat up. I balled my hands up into fists and tried not to shake.

'I already knew all that.'

Draper laughed, 'Be honest Danny, even if it gets her into the country – do you think your marriage is going to last?'

I looked at Ayamin. Tried to breathe deep.

'I do.'

'And if she'd freely choose to marry and associate with a convicted criminal and assist him with breaking the law here and in foreign countries do you think Mrs Yacoub is the sort of person we want in the U.K?'

A snarl appeared on his face as he finished his sentence.

'I do.'

'Why?'

'Because I grew up here. I'm a product of the English foster families, the English schooling system, and I'm a product of the English justice system.' I gestured to the court around me, 'I stole alcohol from a hard-working liquor store owner – I ran away from a Red Cross programme that was supposed to change my ways. I'm a thief, an escapee, I'm a nasty piece of work, but so are you bulldog.'

There was a gasp from the media benches. I laughed like a maniac.

'Mr Frey, we do not allow personal attacks in the courtroom,' the judge began, but I just grinned and ploughed on.

'You steal people's dreams, bulldog. Maybe their lives too... do you ever think about the people that get sent back? The hopelessness they must feel. You're stealing human rights – to safety, to shelter. I think we don't just need Ayamin here in the U.K, we need more people like her – people who just want the things we take for granted.'

The judge's gavel came down.

'If you speak one more word Mr Frey, I'll have you thrown out.'

I glared at Draper. His forehead was red and his fists clenched the pen and paper in his hands. From the corner of my eye, I could see Estelle trying not to laugh.

'Now Mr Frey,' the judge said, taking off her glasses and resting them on the table in front of her, 'I have one more question for you. If you can refrain from slandering anyone here in court today, I shall ask it. Otherwise, you can leave.'

I bit my lip and looked at Ayamin. She was just sitting in her bench wearing her yellow coat. In that moment I stopped caring about Draper or anyone else in court. I was there for Ayamin – all that mattered was her getting into the country.

'I'll answer it.'

Something in my voice must've convinced her because she nodded.

'Mr Frey. Did you really think you could abuse the principles and sacredness of marriage just to try get Mrs Yacoub into the country?'

I thought for a moment, and my eyes wandered from the judge to Ayamin, to Draper, McCurdy, Estelle...

'Mr Frey... Are you going to answer my question?'

I nodded to the judge, 'I'm sorry... I was just thinking about the purpose of marriage – Isn't it to signify love?'

The judge nodded, and I continued.

'If you show you love someone by buying them roses, what have you sacrificed? Fifty quid? An hour of your time?

'What about walking with someone from Turkey to England? What have you sacrificed for your love?' I looked down at my calloused hands, then back up at the court, 'You sacrifice months of your time, broken ribs, drowning, freezing, hunger...'

I pointed to Ayamin, '*What about loving a criminal?* – When she came back to me in France Ayamin potentially sacrificed her chance at making it to England. No police were looking for her, she risked her freedom by throwing her lot in with me. She risked her chance at a trial without the bias of being linked with a criminal.

We're young. We've got a life of mistakes and opportunities ahead of us – A lot of people our age would say we sacrificed our individual freedom by getting married, but I love Ayamin enough to say those vows and commit to a life with her if it means she has a better chance of staying in England.'

****

The court was quiet. Draper was looking much less red, Estelle was staring at me with wide eyes, and Ayamin was smiling.

The judge picked up her glasses, dusted them with a cloth from her pocket and put them back over her eyes.

'Usually, I'd disappear into the backroom to make my decision, but that would mean Mr Frey would have to be taken back to confinement and I'm sure he'd appreciate hearing the decision first hand.'

The judge sighed.

'Ayamin Yacoub, I hope you enjoyed your time in England, because as far as the law is concerned...' the judge paused, and the entire court leaned forwards. I saw the hope, and then bitter despair that played across Ayamin's face, all in a second.

'... Ayamin Yacoub, you can stay as long as you like. We will accept you as a refugee.'

****

Epilogue

I ended up being sentenced to twelve months in jail – proper jail thanks to the fact I'd turned eighteen somewhere along our journey.

The judge who sentenced me said I got six months for my initial sentence, a further five months for evading the police, and an extra month for (accidentally) knocking Gus the court security guard unconscious when I jumped over the stand to try to hug Ayamin.

Gus was fine with it though – he even came and visited me in prison – I said I owed him a beer or two when I got out.

Still. Prison must've had some effect on me. Last week I went before the parole board. They told me I was being let go three months early – good behaviour apparently.

One of my wardens said I was a 'model prisoner' and put my success down to their new prisoner training regime.

I told the parole board the real reason I'd behaved so well – I couldn't put up with seeing Ayamin only once a week any longer.

I'm writing this on my first day out of prison while I catch the number two bus to the East Angles Polytechnic where Ayamin is studying.

They've given her a special course where she can train to be a nurse and finish high school at the same time. It's much harder than a normal course – but she's Ayamin – what more do I need to say?

While I was in prison, I organised a job for myself – stacking shelves at a supermarket. I start work on Friday, and next week Ayamin and I are going to look at a flat together.

It's not that flash, or in the most scenic location, but it has a yellow door and it comes with a second-hand Vespa scooter. *I hope we get it.*

My bus is pulling into the polytechnic now. I can already see Ayamin waiting. God she's beautiful.

Tonight, we're going to have fish and chips by the ocean to celebrate. We talked about going to a flash restaurant – but the ocean's more our style. Plus, it means we're saving a little more for our summer road trip through Europe.

The bus has stopped. Ayamin's waving at me. I don't think I'll ever get over her smile.

It's funny, all the papers said our story had a happy ending – in some ways I guess they're right – but at the same time, I feel like our story is just beginning.

On quitting jobs and sleeping rough (AUTHOR'S NOTE)

This book took a long time to write. I quit my job twice to work on it, left my flat and spent a few months living on friends' floors and in the back of a van.

But if I ever questioned why I was devoting so much time to this book I only needed to type 'Syria' into Google. The stories of men, women, and children – actual people having their lives torn apart through the insanity of other humans would appear before me.

You're awesome for reading this book. You're awesome if you go off and act on any feelings you had throughout – kindness really is a lantern in this sometimes-dark world.

- Elijah Hill

www.ingramcontent.com/pod-product-compliance
Ingram Content Group UK Ltd.
Pitfield, Milton Keynes, MK11 3LW, UK
UKHW021036270726
13967UKWH00013B/2807

9 780473 597856